# I'm standing smack in the center of his office

when the silhouette of a tall man fills the doorway. The hard planes of his cheekbones give his gorgeous face a European elegance, but his unshaven jaw gives off the air of a rugged mountain man. And while he's wearing a sleek black suit and burgundy-colored tie, there's something about him—perhaps the way he's standing with a ramrod straight back and a noticeable bulk in his arms—that tells me he is not a fine-suit man. He vibes ex-Marine or some other tough-guy type profession.

Our gazes lock, and it's then that I notice his unusual light gray eyes. They're stunning, and I can't look away. Surprisingly, he seems equally mesmerized, because he's just standing there with an odd expression.

*Lust?*

*No. Not possible.* Maybe he recognizes me, though that isn't likely.

Abruptly, the moment shatters, and his expression shifts to a nasty scowl like he's caught himself doing something he shouldn't.

"What are you standing there looking at?" He shoves his cell phone in his pant pocket.

## PRAISE FOR THE OHELLNO SERIES

"This was a book that had me literally laughing out loud. More than once. Which is something I've come to expect from Mimi Jean Pamfiloff's romantic comedies."

**—Sara, Harlequin Junkies, on *SMART TASS***

"What I love about this book is what I love about most of the books that I have read by this author. It is the witty banter, the snarky comments and the connection between the two main characters."

**—Three Chicks and Their Books, on *SMART TASS***

"I seriously LOVE Mimi Jean Pamfiloff's talented writing style so much that I can add her to my addiction list."

**—Jennifer Person, The Power of Three Readers, on *SMART TASS***

OH HENRY. "This story was sexy and sweet, a dose of fun with the signature Mimi-snark."

**—Leigh, Guilty Pleasures Book Reviews**

"Oh, Henry!!! It's sweet, funny, and oh so sexy. A definite FIVE-STAR read that has the three H's: HILARITY, HOTNESS, and HEART. The amazingly talented Ms. Pamfiloff has written your next book boyfriend, Henry Walton. Get ready to fall in love with this cocky unfiltered athlete and his quirky smartass match, Elle! You will love their banter and his quest to win her over."

### —Bestselling author of *Until Alex*, J. Nathan

"Mimi Jean Pamfiloff has topped even herself! Wonderful characters, some truly twisted events and some pretty awesome reading as two people learn to work as partners and trust in one another for support!"

### —Tome Tender, on *OH HENRY*

"*Oh Henry* ratcheted everything up a notch. Still some sweet romance, some very funny situations, and a little bit of angst as both Elle and Henry are dealing with some serious issues. And, what would a Mimi Jean book be without one of her little added twists."

### —Carol's Reviews

# OTHER WORKS BY MIMI JEAN PAMFILOFF

**COMING SOON!**
Check (Part 3, Mr. Rook's Island Series)
The Librarian's Vampire Assistant, Book 2

**THE ACCIDENTALLY YOURS SERIES**
(Paranormal Romance/Humor)
Accidentally in Love with…a God? (Book 1)
Accidentally Married to…a Vampire? (Book 2)
Sun God Seeks…Surrogate? (Book 3)
Accidentally…Evil? (a Novella) (Book 3.5)
Vampires Need Not…Apply? (Book 4)
Accidentally…Cimil? (a Novella) (Book 4.5)
Accidentally…Over? (Series Finale) (Book 5)

**THE FATE BOOK SERIES**
(Standalones/New Adult Suspense/Humor)
Fate Book
Fate Book Two

**THE FUGLY SERIES**
(Standalones/Contemporary Romance)
fugly
it's a fugly life

**THE HAPPY PANTS SERIES**
(Standalones/Romantic Comedy)
The Happy Pants Café (Prequel)
Tailored for Trouble (Book 1)
Leather Pants (Book 2)
Skinny Pants (Book 3)

**IMMORTAL MATCHMAKERS, INC., SERIES**
(Standalones/Paranormal/Humor)
The Immortal Matchmakers (Book 1)
Tommaso (Book 2)
God of Wine (Book 3)
The Goddess of Forgetfulness (Book 4)

**THE KING SERIES**
(Dark Fantasy)
King's (Book 1)
King for a Day (Book 2)
King of Me (Book 3)
Mack (Book 4)
Ten Club (Series Finale, Book 5)

**THE LIBRARIAN'S VAMPIRE ASSISTANT**
(Mystery/Humor)
The Librarian's Vampire Assistant (Book 1)

**THE MERMEN TRILOGY**
(Dark Fantasy)
Mermen (Book 1)
MerMadmen (Book 2)
MerCiless (Book 3)

**MR. ROOK'S ISLAND SERIES**
(Romantic Suspense)
Mr. Rook (Part 1)
Pawn (Part 2)

**THE OHELLNO SERIES**
(Standalones/New Adult/Romantic Comedy)
Smart Tass (Book 1)
Oh Henry (Book 2)
Digging A Hole (Book 3) <-You are here. ☺

# DIGGING A HOLE

## The OHellNO Series
## Book 3

## Mimi Jean Pamfiloff

*A Mimi Boutique Novel*

# DIGGING A HOLE

# CHAPTER ONE

"I can't believe it. Sydney Lucas is a bigger loser than me." I groan as I talk into my cell and yank off my blonde wig from the safety of my bathroom.

"Uh-oh. I'm guessing the interview didn't go so well?" says Abigail on the other end of the line. She's been my best friend since middle school and is the only person on the planet who knows what I, the infamously shy Georgie Walton, have been up to these past two weeks: an epic scandal in the making.

If I ever get caught.

Which I won't.

"You guessed correctly. The interview was a disaster." I sigh and turn away from my annoying reflection in the mirror, planting my ass on the marble counter. "I literally threw up on the woman's shoes."

"No. You didn't." Abi sounds like she's going to laugh but holds back. She's a good friend. She's also a down-to-earth and timid-as-hell brunette like me. Only, I've been living a double life lately, thus the crazy blonde wig and hipster glasses.

"Did," I say. "I had oatmeal for breakfast, too. It was a sticky mess—complete with theatrical heaving."

"Wow, girl," says Abi. "You've really upped your game; you only got nauseous at the last nine interviews."

"Well, ten must be my lucky number, because after I heaved, I was so embarrassed, I nearly passed out, which then made me more humiliated so I just ran from the room crying. Which is why I'm done."

"No. You can't quit, Georgie. This is too important, and if you give up now, you'll never believe you can stand on your own two feet."

At this point, you might be asking if I'm mental, and maybe I am; however, the root of the problem comes down to one thing. I am deathly shy and have been since the age of five. I can't pinpoint the exact moment it started, but I'm fairly sure it began when I realized my family wasn't your everyday American family. I remember going out with my mother one day and being followed by dozens of news trucks. "Georgie," my mom said, "always be on your guard. They're watching."

"Who, Mommy?" I'd asked.

"Everyone."

From that moment on, I've always felt claustrophobic, enclosed in some musty, dark closet, the cold walls suffocating me, making it harder and harder to breathe. That closet is the world. *Yep. I'm totally mental.*

"I don't know, Abi," I say, "I thought I could pull this off, yanno? But no matter what I do, I can't get through a goddamned interview." And if I can't do that, then what's the point of my life? To be a freakishly awkward woman-child who has to rely on her siblings?

No.

This is *my* life.

And getting a job is my chance to change how my family sees me—the timid, incapable twenty-one-year-old baby of our family who will never do anything more than stand in a shadowy corner, hiding from the world.

*I know I am more than that.* However, the words I think aren't backed up with action, and every time I fail, my self-worth drops a notch. This moment is do or die. It's win or lose. It's my coming to Jesus.

*Ugh. Only, I just threw up on his sandals.* Metaphorically speaking, of course.

"I'm done, Abi. I thought pretending to be someone else would take off the pressure of being a Walton, but Sydney Lucas is just as bad at dealing with people as I am."

Abi sighs on the other end of the phone. "Georgie, please don't give up. You can land an internship. I know you can."

"With who? I've tried every company with business internships in the Houston area."

"Another position just opened up at PVP. You could work with me."

My brother is actually the person who recommended Abi for the role. Palo Verde Pharmaceuticals is a multibillion-dollar company owned by my family and is ironically tied to the reason that I absolutely must stand on my own two feet. Simply put, my family's billions in assets are in the midst of an ugly and very public legal battle. Okay. Let me rephrase. My siblings and I are suing my father for control of Walton Holdings, which owns twenty large companies.

Yep. You heard me right. It's a kiddie coup. Only, we're not kids and it has nothing to do with greed, but everything to do with money. Yeah. It's complicated. Take the IRS tax code, triple that, and you'd have my situation.

Nevertheless, we cannot fail, which means it's up to my siblings to win, and they must demonstrate the companies are in good hands if we run them. Sadly, we're shorthanded of people we can trust. Every executive, government agency, greedy lawyer, vulture, and thief in a suit is trying to angle their way into this mess, hoping to influence the outcome and benefit their own interests. Bottom line: Oil is a big business. And my family *is* the oil business. In fact, we're Texas oil, which makes us even bigger in our Texan minds. But it's why I must step in and help. Running twenty companies is just too massive for my brother, sisters, and sister-in-law.

First things first, however; I have to show my older siblings that I'm capable so they'll let me work in the family company.

"So how 'bout it?" Abi pushes. "Not like any of the employees will ever recognize you. You've never had anything to do with the operations, and most people only know your father and brother."

I give it a little thought. Maybe she's right. My father is the titan of Walton Holdings, so it's mostly his face people associate with our family, followed by my brother, Henry, who's all over the TV and sports magazines because he's an up-and-coming NFL superstar. But more than that, he's been given temporary control of my family's companies during this time of crisis. Well, really, it's him and his super-genius wife, Elle, who is the sweetest, nerdiest girl I've ever met. If you took a tele-transporter that was fueled by puppy breath and baby giggles, that would be Elle. Smart, cute, and amazingly compassionate.

"I don't know," I say. "I think at least the executives might recognize me. My dad usually has our family photo in the back of their annual company reports."

"Which nobody looks at," Abi argues. "Plus you're such a hermit that any pictures of you floating around are obscured by your long brown hair, which you're going to dye blonde and pull out of your face."

"What about my wig and glasses?" I ask.

"Drop it. They look crazy suspicious—like a cross between Waldo and a floor mop."

"Now you tell me." I've gone on ten interviews with my "golden curls of seduction" wig and chunky glasses, hoping to look more outgoing and cool.

"I didn't want to discourage you, but now I'm encouraging you; PVP is the perfect solution."

Interning at a company I partially own? *It sounds like a PR disaster waiting to happen.* "I think I'll keep looking."

"Georgie, the final interviews are tomorrow."

"And?" I ask.

"And let's pretend you look for something else. Maybe you look for two or three more weeks and you still come up empty-handed. This position will be gone."

"Abi, you're not the hiring manager, so it's not like you can just give me the job."

"True. But I can put in a good word with Rebecca, my boss, and she can mention my praise to Nick Brooks."

"Who's that?" Not that it matters. I'm not changing my mind.

"The hiring manager. He's the new VP of sales, a genius, and the devil incarnate. The worst human being I've ever—"

"Such a selling point. Passing," I sing.

"You didn't let me finish. He may be the biggest a-hole to ever walk the planet, but anyone who works for him is deemed an instant god—sky's the limit for their future. I even heard that the team from his old job are all VPs at different companies now."

An image of my father instantly comes to mind. He's such an epic bastard that merely working for him and surviving is almost the equivalent of having a Harvard degree when it comes to résumés. Not that my father ever dreamed of allowing his children to attend such a "despicable" school in a place that isn't Texas. "*Texas made us who we are, and over my dead body will my children attend a university in some other state. It's our obligation as Waltons to show pride in our institutions.*"

Now, before anyone runs off thinking that he can't be all that bad for his loyalty and love of state, let me translate what he really means: "We're as rich as sin and more powerful than God because we have every politician, judge, and state agency in our pocket. We wouldn't want to ruffle feathers by appearing unsupportive of our fine universities." He expects us to play our public part because being a Walton is all about power. And keeping it. It also means that convincing a jury of my father's mental incompetence will be impossible. Impossifuckingble. He's got way too many allies. Still, we have to try. The alternative is losing everything to an insane yoga cult.

Yoga.

Cult.

There, I said it.

Yes, yes. #WTAF. What the almighty fuck? I'll

get to yoga-cult-explaining in a moment, but right now I've got to make a big choice.

"So this VP," I ask, "how good is he?"

"If a Häagen-Dazs ice cream bar fucked a Twinkie and they had a baby, then you deep-fried that baby in donut batter and rolled it in a mixture of rainbow sprinkles and winning lotto tickets, you'd have Nick Brooks."

"He sounds fattening."

"Ohellno. He doesn't sleep, and he expects his team to be equally immortal. You'll drop ten pounds on the first day. We've already seen a thirty percent bump in sales, and he's only been with the company a few months."

*Hmm...* I'm starting to like the idea. I mean, my family's companies—whether it's oil, renewable energy, or pharma—depend on sales. So working for a big sales VP would not only prove I'm more than just a shy little girl incapable of contributing anything to this world, but I might learn something useful to help my family. *But how the hell will I survive the interview?*

"Please, Georgie? Please?" Abi begs. "We could eat lunch together every day. I can help you with anything that gets in your way, and you can help me."

Abigail is shy but doesn't need my help. She's been finding her way just fine this last year, heading up several organizations at the university we attend here in Houston. Shyness may have brought us together, but she's left me in the dust. Still, just knowing she'll be by my side if I get the internship might be the lucky charm I need.

"Okay. I'll interview," I say, thinking I'm going to need to make an appointment for my hair tonight. My sister Claire, who's a super-girly girl and summer-highlights addict, has someone on call—Fabiana—so I'll try her.

"Yay!" Abi cheers. "I'll text you the details."

"Thanks, Abi. But please don't get your hopes up." I pause. "Well, unless you're hoping I'll pass out. Then your prayers might be answered."

"Georgie, just think—"

"Sydney," I correct. "You can't forget to use my fake name."

"Sorry. Sydney, just think positive."

"Why wouldn't I? Not like anything could possibly go wrong with using a false identity to work at a company I practically own." *And if you believe that, I have a unicorn to sell you.*

# CHAPTER TWO

*Four and a Half Months Earlier.*

"Dad, what's happening?" my older sister Claire asks as our private jet, bound for Miami, seems to be dropping altitude quickly.

I look up from my window seat, where I've been busy studying for my statistics final coming right before winter break in about a week. Honestly, I don't even know why my father, the infamous Chester Walton, insisted we all come on this trip. I've got a ton of classwork, and it's not like he needs me for any of these public appearances.

I don't speak.

I don't even appear.

I just stand in the background, hoping to God no one notices me, and they usually don't.

Speaking of noticing, now that I'm paying attention, the plane is dropping a little fast, but we've been in the air for almost four hours, so it's probably just time to land.

My father, whose seat faces us, is relaxing and

reading a paper, which only confirms nothing's wrong. Except, when I glance over at Claire again, her usually pale face is terror-white.

"Dad?" Michelle prods, looking equally petrified. She's the second oldest and two years younger than Claire, who's twenty-six. Henry comes third on the totem pole of siblings, though he's off at some out-of-state football game. Not like he would've come had my father asked, since those two do not get along. My dad always envisioned all his children working by his side in the family business, but Henry has his sights set on the NFL.

Sitting beside me and white-knuckling the armrest, my mother, Georgina—who I'm named after—looks worried too. For the record, my sisters and I all look like her with our brown hair, medium heights and builds, and big eyes, except mine aren't brown. They're green like my father's and Henry's, the two blonds of our family. Girls brown. Men blond.

"Chester?" my mother says. "Go check with the pilot and see what's happening."

My father keeps his perma-frown directed at the paper. "There's nothing to worry about, dear." He folds the paper in order to get at the lower half.

"This is ridiculous." My mother unbuckles her seatbelt and gets up to go ask the pilot herself. As she passes, my father's hand whips out and catches her wrist.

"Sit. Down. Georgina," he growls. "I also suggest you fasten your seatbelts. Immediately."

Standing sideways and facing my father, my mother blinks. I can't tell what she's thinking, but she must know something I don't because she goes from looking concerned to looking petrified—brows pulled tightly together, brown eyes wide, face sheet white.

"No. Chester, no. You promised," she hisses.

With a sinister look in his eyes, my dad beats her down with a single word. "Sit." My father can say a lot with just his tone. It's a skill he's acquired over many years of cutthroat business tactics that have made our family one of the wealthiest in the country. These last few years he's been diversifying into green energy and pharmaceuticals—miracle drugs specifically. But don't let that fool you. He's all about the money. It's his life. And if he gets to crush skulls while making it, even better in his mind.

I watch my mother return to her seat, pointy chin held high. She's trying to hide her emotions, but the quivering bottom lip gives her away.

"Mom?" I turn to her, speaking in my quietest voice. "What's happening?"

Her hand slides over the armrest and pats my leg. "Your father has lost his marbles, and I believe he's kidnapping us."

"Huh?" I turn my entire body in her direction. I'm not sure I heard her correctly.

"Children." She clears her throat, glaring at my

father like she wants to rip out his soulless green eyes. "Please know that I have nothing to do with this. Your father has not been feeling well lately and is supposed to be on medication. I'm sorry I didn't tell you, but he promised to take his pills and apparently changed his mind."

*Whatthewhat?*

"Mom? Dad? What the hell are you talking about?" Claire looks like she's about to be sick.

Meanwhile, I finally look out my window and notice the ocean. And I don't mean it's twenty thousand feet below us. I see white caps and waves almost at eye level.

*Oh shit!* We're going to hit the water.

I open my mouth to say something, but the plane slams forward and everything goes dark.

# CHAPTER THREE

*Present Day.*

*Don't pass out. Your family needs you. Don't pass out.
Your family needs—*

"Sydney!" I hear Abi squeal from across the lobby, where I'm sitting with seventeen other applicants, who I assume are all students like myself, hoping to snag the coveted Nick Brooks paid internship.

We're all wearing our best ill-fitting adult clothes—you know, the kind most students buy off the rack from a discount clothing store that makes us cringe because we're spending what little we have to look like our parents. Or at least to look responsible enough to convince someone to give us a job. But, of course, my clothes are Neiman's finest from my sister Claire's closet—her hand-me-downs. Not that I can't afford expensive clothes, but she loves to shop and wear nice things. Once. Whereas I must be forced to buy clothes, and when I do, they never meet my mom's approval. Long comfortable knit skirts or jeans, T-shirts, flip-flops. I'm an Old Navy poster child. Cheap Target sweats and shorts are great, too. "Not to Walton standards, Georgie," my mom always says. But she knows the only way I'll wear mom-approved clothes is if they come from Claire since I hate waste. I'm so green that the trees are jealous, a result, no doubt, of my guilt over our oil fortune. Okay, and maybe watching *WALL-E* too many times when I was about ten. I figure, though, that someday I'll get over this curse of being overly self-conscious and timid, and when I do, I'll use my wealth to do something good for the world.

I stand and watch Abi sashay across the white marble floor of the sprawling lobby that has huge windows and pale gray walls. Her brown hair is pulled back into a ponytail, and she's in a plain black suit and white button-down blouse. Coincidentally, my exact same outfit and hairdo. Only now I'm a honey blonde.

"Hi, Abigail." I extend my hand. "It's a pleasure to see you again."

She catches on that I don't want everyone to know we're close friends. Because we're not. *Georgie* is her friend. I'm Sydney Lucas. Smart, outgoing, and from a regular family who is not currently trying to have their father declared legally insane for kidnapping his children and wife last year and then subjecting them to cruel and very unusual yoga.

Abi winks. "Yes. Such a pleasure to see you again, Miss Lucas." She shakes my hand, stifling a smile. "Please follow me."

I notice the other interviewees discreetly sizing me up. *And cue jitters, stomach cramps, and rapid breathing.* It's all part of this big, glorious, scary-ass package known as me.

I follow Abi past the turnstiles, where she scans in, and we head to the elevators. There are five on each side, ten total.

"Jesus, this place is huge." Much bigger than I'd imagined and almost the same size as our corporate headquarters across town.

We step inside an empty elevator, and the moment the doors close, Abi turns and grabs me by the shoulders. "Get a hold of yourself, Georgie." She gives me a hard shake. "You're turning green."

"I can't breathe," I rasp out.

"Well, you'd better, because I spent twenty minutes this morning telling Mr. Brooks all about you. Do you have any idea how hard that was for me?"

"No?" I whimper.

She shakes me again. "I almost peed myself!"

"Oh no. Is he that bad?"

She blinks. "No. Okay. Yes. He's the worst. And on top of that, he's hot. Remember Mike from our junior year?"

How could I forget? He was six two or three, with the body of an Olympic god, and hazel eyes you could get lost in. *So beautiful...* I sigh and nod.

"Well, Nick Brooks is ten times hotter. But he's

sharp. And he's a fucking ogre—makes the Grim Reaper look like Professor Booboo the hipster guinea pig."

For the life of me I can't understand why she's ambushing me with this information.

"I can't do it." I start hyperventilating and poking the *Open Door* button so I can run away and hide on whatever floor Mr. Brooks isn't.

"No! I stuck my neck out for you, Georgie. You can't bail."

I turn with clenched fists. "Why did you do that? You knew I'd fuck this up!"

"Shut your piehole, girl. We're in this together now, and in ten seconds those doors will open, and you have to nail it." She shakes me again so hard that my teeth clack. "So get your shit together!"

I nod dumbly, trying to absorb the magnitude of the situation. For whatever idiotic reason, Abi has hitched her wagon to mine. Blind faith? Stupidity? Doesn't matter why now; what's done is done.

"Okay. I can do this. I know I can." I pant.

"Good. But whatever you do," Abi adds, "don't look at the floor, okay? Direct eye contact only. Brooks has a reputation for weeding out the weak from the herd."

"Are you trying to make me feel better or worse?" Because we both know if we were a herd of elk roaming the tundra, I'd be the limping doe trailing a mile behind the rest with a giant "eat me" sign on my ass.

"Look," she says, "if I can handle speaking to him for twenty minutes, you can handle ten. Just breathe through your nose, smile, and remember that if you fuck this up, I'll look like an imbecile."

The elevator slows, and I feel my stomach tightening. My head starts to spin. *Oh God.* But I know how badly Abi needs a full-time job after college. Her father died years ago, and her mother's interior design business isn't doing so well. She mortgaged her house to pay for Abi's tuition, so Abi can't afford to be unemployed when she graduates next year. This paid internship is her gateway to an impressive résumé, solid reference, and a good-paying job to help her mother.

"I won't let you down," I say, wondering why the hell I let her talk me into this. It's a horrible risk for her. But that's Abi; she's always stuck her neck out for me, yet she refuses to take help from anyone. Stubborn to the core.

If Mr. Brooks is anything like the scent in his office, I'm in trouble. Imagine the smell of power—leather and expensive spices—mixed with the light earthiness of an unlit cigar and the faint aroma of coffee, no doubt from the steaming cup sitting on his immaculate, solid oak desk.

*Wait, is that a hint of blood I smell, too?* No. Just my imagination. And right now, it's visualizing a horrible beast with dripping red fangs coming my way.

As I wait and wait and wait some more for Mr. Brooks and his devil horns to make an appearance, I distract myself with taking inventory of his office. I'm surprised to see he has no personal effects except for a small plant on the windowsill behind his desk. On one wall he has a large clean whiteboard and some framed degrees and awards.

I walk over to check them out. *Wow. Impressive.* MBA from Yale, degree in finance from Northwestern, and a salesperson of the quarter award. Abi wasn't joking. Nick Brooks hasn't been with the company even a year, and he's already their top sales VP.

I turn on my heel, wondering what makes a man like him tick and what might possibly make him go easy on a weak elk. I turn to face the shelving at the far end of the room near the open door. There are lots and lots of white binders, likely filled with reports or something, but again I see zero personal photos.

*Not even of a pet?* He's either antisocial, very private, or intolerable and no one likes to be around him.

Suddenly, outside the open door, I hear a deep voice yelling in the hallway.

"Ask me if I fucking care!" the man roars in a deep, authoritative voice. "I'll give you until five today, and then we're pulling every pill, bottle, and goddamned sample from your shelves, got it?"

I'm standing smack in the center of his office when the silhouette of a tall man fills the doorway. The hard planes of his cheekbones give his gorgeous face a European elegance, but his unshaven jaw gives off the air of a rugged mountain man. And while he's wearing a sleek black suit and burgundy-colored tie, there's something about him—perhaps the way he's standing with a ramrod straight back and a noticeable bulk in his arms—that tells me he is not a fine-suit man. He vibes ex-Marine or some other tough-guy type profession.

Our gazes lock, and it's then that I notice his unusual light gray eyes. They're stunning, and I can't look away. Surprisingly, he seems equally mesmerized, because he's just standing there with an odd expression.

*Lust?*

*No. Not possible.* Maybe he recognizes me, though that isn't likely.

Abruptly, the moment shatters, and his expression shifts to a nasty scowl like he's caught himself doing something he shouldn't.

"What are you standing there looking at?" He shoves his cell phone in his pant pocket.

I attempt to open my mouth, not that I expect actual words to come out, but he cuts me off before I'm allowed to blubber. *Thank God.*

"Oh. You're that intern everyone's been pushing up my ass." He sails past me, going to his desk, and

I catch a whiff of his cologne, which smells like leather and sage, which is oddly fitting. He looks to be in his early thirties. Leather is classic while sage is a trendier scent this year.

"Well, can you type?" he asks with a curt tone, riffling through his desk and not bothering to look at me.

"Ye-yes?" I manage to squeak out.

"Can you pour coffee?"

"Well?" he grumbles, pulling out several manila folders and plunking them on his desk next to the coffee.

"Uh, yes. I p-pour coffee."

"Then you start Monday. Now, get out. I'm busy."

"Uhhhh…I got the job?" But he hasn't asked me anything about my résumé.

Slowly, those silvery cold eyes lift from the folder in his hands. The stark bitterness in his gaze makes me want to run for the hills and forget I ever met him. *No. Your family needs you.* And now, Abi is counting on me.

"Why are you still standing there?" he rumbles quietly.

I begin backing out of his office, palms raised in the universal gesture of "don't hurt me."

"Close the damned door on your way out." He picks up the phone on his desk, and the moment I shut the door, that deep, malevolent voice roars through the walls. His door does nothing to mute the thunderous tone.

I whoosh out a breath. *What the hell was that?* I feel like my heart's about to explode, it's beating so fast. And my head is spinning like a clothes dryer on the hyperventilation cycle.

"Sydney?"

I turn to see Abi standing there, a hopeful look in her light brown eyes. "So? Did you get it?"

I nod. "Yeah. I think so."

She jumps and squeals. "Yay! Yay! I knew it."

While she's rejoicing, my mind is catching up to the reality of the situation. I grab her by the elbow and drag her down the hall to the first open door I see, marked conference room 1230b. I yank her inside and give her a shake. "What the fuck, Abi! Why would you set me up for an interview with that monster?"

"Calm down. I mean, yeah, the man is a giant medieval barbarian masquerading as an underwear model, and most of us would like to scratch his eyes out. But! But! We'd equally like to fuck the hell out of him, too, and no one will argue that he isn't a genius, so the kind of stuff you'll learn is immeasurable."

"While I'd gladly give up my virginity or sit on the face of a man who *looks* like him, he seems to be lacking a fucking soul! I can't work for him—he's horrible."

She snarls with her light brown eyes and bellies up. "You can and you will."

I press my stomach to hers with equal measure. "You're out of your fucking mind."

The door flies open, and standing there is the a-hole himself, Nick Brooks, a look of displeasure in his silvery eyes.

*Uh-oh…* I gulp.

"What are you two clowns doing in here?" he snarls.

Abi looks at me, then at him, then at me again. "We were just…we were just…" Abi can't seem to come up with an explanation. Meanwhile, I'm frozen in place.

He narrows his eyes. "How about having your little gossip session elsewhere? Because I sincerely doubt that anyone in this room could give two shits about anything you have to say."

*Room? Anyone?* Abi and I turn our heads to my right and take in the view of the faces seated around the executive table at the far, far end of the room.

*Oh crap.* My stomach cramps up, and my head starts feeling like it's in a vise. Approximately nine women and men in suits are staring at us.

Abi chuckles nervously. "Uh, sorry, folks. We, uh…" She grabs my hand and yanks me around Brooks, out into the hall, forcing me to run until we're at the stairwell. The moment we reach it, I double over.

"I think I'm going to pass out," I groan.

"Oh, God! Not now, Georgie!"

I can't help it. My nervous system has reached

my max. *Overload. Overload!* Luckily, I was too scared of repeating the oatmeal episode, so I skipped breakfast.

I will myself to stand, wiping the sweat from my brow with the back of my hand.

Abi looks at me and starts laughing. After a long moment, I laugh, too, but mostly out of embarrassment.

"You got the job!" She bounces on the balls of her feet.

"I can't work for him, Abi. He'll eat me alive and crap me out." I let out a slow breath.

"Georgie," she sighs with disappointment, "this is the moment you've been waiting for."

To work for some asshole who treats me like a doormat? *Me thinks not.* "If I wanted to be told I'm worthless and stupid, I could just spend more time with my father." Of course, that's not exactly true anymore. My father, once the world's most cold-hearted, money-grubbing billionaire, now spends his days lighting incense and doing the downward dog in the buff. He also speaks to animals. And bugs. And trees. The man's lost it. Still, I've spent twenty-one years of my life being written off by him and everyone around me, including my brother, Henry, and my two sisters, Michelle and Claire, who genuinely care but don't have high expectations due to my panic issues. My mother, Georgina, is slightly more supportive, but in her very reserved, hard-nosed way. *You can do better, so do it* is her favorite thing to say.

"No, Georgie." Abi grips my arm. "You're missing the point. Brooks is your dragon. He's everything you've ever feared."

"Meaning," I nod slowly, "I'm supposed to slay him." It's the lamest idea she's ever come up with.

"You need to learn to stand up for yourself, Georgie."

"I know, but—"

"But nothing. Haven't you ever wondered how I turned the corner?" She points toward the door. "I had some asshole boss just like him when I worked at Taco World last summer, and he was the best thing to ever happen to me. I became immune to him after a few weeks. Then no one could scare me. Of course, he was stupid, so I didn't learn anything, but Brooks is smart. You keep your eyes and ears open, and you'll walk out of here knowing everything about sales."

I stare at the cement floor, the orange fluorescent lighting of the stairwell casting gloomy shadows all around us. It feels like I'm deciding whether or not to enter hell and work for Satan. *For the experience and personal growth, of course.* That said, I've tried everything to overcome this mental hurdle—hypnosis, therapy, visualization, antianxiety drugs, meditation, and emotional support teddy bears since my dad would never let me have a real pet. *Maybe it's time to try a dragon.*

"Georgie," she pushes, "you don't have any other job offers, and you can quit anytime, so just give it a try. What do you have to lose?"

I start thinking of my family and how much they need me. I have a lot to lose. And so do they.

"Okay. Fine."

She claps and lets out another squeal. "I'm so excited!"

I wish I could share her enthusiasm, especially now that I've apparently confessed to the PVP leadership team that I'm a virgin who'd gladly sit on Brooks's face if he had a soul.

"Okay. Let's get you over to HR to start your paperwork."

I shake my head. "I can't do that. Fake name, remember?"

"I thought Robbie got you set up." Robbie is a guy we met in our computer science class. He's one of those genius geeky types who earns cash by selling fake driver's licenses.

"He doesn't do Social Security cards, but don't worry. I'll figure something out." I practically grew up in places like these. The Walton Holdings' building is like Fort Knox, yet I still manage to get in there without anything. And no, the security guards there never recognize me. I'm utterly forgettable. In any case, my bigger concern right now is keeping the job long enough to prove I'm more than just a shy face, while working for the meanest boss ever to walk the earth.

*Georgie*, I remind myself, *you've been through a lot worse*. And I can't ever forget that if it weren't for me, my mother and sisters might not be alive today. I know I have it in me to be strong.

# CHAPTER FOUR

*Approximately Four and a Half Months Earlier.*

Tears and snot run down my wet face as I watch the tail of our plane sink into the Gulf of Mexico. My sister Claire has a gash on the side of her head, and my mother is doing her best to stop the bleeding with her sweater. Everyone is yelling and screaming at my father.

"This is for the best. You'll see," he says, a wild look in his eyes.

My ears are still ringing from the plane's hard landing in the ocean, but I swear I hear someone yelling off in the distance. My head hurts, and everything feels like a bad confusing dream, the faces around me distorted. However, I'm lucid enough to know that no one else hears the distress call.

Slowly, I turn and squint in the direction of the late afternoon sun to the west. Off in the distance, I spot a head bobbing in the waves.

I quickly look around our large yellow raft. All

are accounted for except the pilot.

I'm about to tell everyone he's there, but then something happens inside me. I see Michelle blubbering hysterically, her long brown hair wet and dripping down her face. I see blood coming from Claire's head, running down my mother's arm and lap as she tries to calm her. My father is gazing off into the distance, a crazed look in his eyes as he keeps repeating he knows what he's doing. And then there's me. I'm in shock. I cannot believe that my father would orchestrate such a horrific event. Had it not been for my fast reflexes and getting that door open, we would all be at the bottom of the ocean this very moment. And for what? Why would he do something so heinous to his own family?

My gaze slowly glides to the tiny head bobbing in the waves, growing smaller with every push of the wind. All I can think is that while my father clearly came up with this idea, the pilot carried out the plan. He purposefully crashed us into the cold ocean, and I'm sure he did it for money. *Greedy coldhearted motherfucker.*

I turn my back to the man and place my hand on Michelle's leg.

"It's okay, Georgie." She pats my forearm. "We're going to get through this."

But we're in the middle of nowhere, surrounded by miles of deep blue water, and I'm guessing my father made sure that our plane isn't going to be found.

He's mad. *We're all going to die.*

It's now pitch black, and we have been in this raft for nearly six hours. No one is speaking, and Claire, my injured sister, is passed out. It's a moment when I begin reflecting on my life and what I might've done differently had I known things would end here.

I sure as hell would've stood up to my father, but I never have, and now I'm asking myself why. Where does the wall inside my head come from? I don't feel weak. I don't feel stupid or worthless either. Yet that's not the person I show to the world. I open my mouth, words primed and ready for articulation, but something always snatches them right from my throat. It's fear, I realize. Fear of everyone turning their heads and looking at me, judging.

"*Careful, Georgie. The world is watching,*" I hear my mother's voice echo inside my head. And maybe they are, but so what? If they stare and disapprove, what will happen? Will the sky fall? Will I shrivel up and die? No. And *this* is exactly what kills me! I know all this! I know in my heart of hearts that nothing bad will happen if I release my inner Georgie. Yet I can't bring myself to do it.

Suddenly, a motor and giant spotlight off in the distance catch my attention. It's a boat heading straight for us.

"Mom, look!" I point. It's a moment of pure joy, knowing we'll be rescued. I just have no idea what my father plans to do. *He's not interested in being saved.*

I'm guessing my mother and Michelle are thinking the same thing because no one is cheering and the tension in the air just spiked.

*I have to push him off the raft.* It's the only way to give everyone else time to get on that boat first and warn the crew what we're dealing with.

The boat draws closer, and I prepare to fling myself on him. I'll go into the water, too, if I have to, but he is not getting on that boat until we're sure we can contain him somehow. *Maybe we'll leave him in the raft and tow him.*

The boat pulls up to us, and I'm about to leap when my father yells, "What the hell took you so long, huh?"

A tall, thin man in tattered cutoffs and a white T-shirt tosses my dad a line. "Sorry, sir."

*This isn't a rescue.* My already freezing body turns ice cold.

Michelle and I look at my mother, who doesn't flinch. She simply starts helping secure the raft so we can get Claire onto the small fishing boat. I don't know for certain, but I'm guessing my mother is biding her time. She is no fool, and like my father, she comes from a long line of callous, calculating people. In fact, our fortune is really my mother's. My father took over her family's oil business after they married. He's grown it into an empire, but we all know it's because my mother allowed him to take the reins. She didn't want the long hours and nonstop work. Her speed is shopping, fundraising, and playing tennis with her friends, but make no mistake, she's equally cunning.

I am the last to leave the raft, and when I step aboard, my father is pointing a rifle in my direction.

*Oh shit.* "Dad! No!" I hold up my hands defensively, sure he's about to put a bullet in my head. I mean, why not? He's clearly insane.

"Georgie, you always were a disappointment, but I'll make something out of you yet."

I look over the tops of my hands as he aims the rifle at the raft and fires.

*Oh. He's sinking it*, I realize.

He shakes his head at me. "Word of advice, Georgie, if anyone ever points a gun at you with the intent to kill, you don't hold back. You lunge straight for that barrel, hit it away, and fight. But you never surrender." He turns and disappears down the dark narrow stairwell below deck.

*This crazy bastard wants to give me life lessons? Surreal.* Which is why I can't shake the feeling that this is all a nightmare and, at any moment, I'll wake up in an ambulance, discovering I survived a plane crash.

# CHAPTER FIVE

*Present Day.*

It's Saturday afternoon, and I'm due at my brother, Henry's for lunch. He still tries to find time for family even though he's been under a ton of pressure studying for finals and preparing for his first year playing pro football. On top of that, he has the media circus to deal with and twenty different companies we're fighting to keep control of.

Luckily, he's not doing any of this alone. Claire is helping with the oil side of things, and Michelle and her husband, Chewy, are managing the PR. Elle, my brother's new wife, who's actually a year younger than me, is running everything else, including working with the army of lawyers we've retained for the battle. We've even teamed up with Henry's university in Austin and hired half a dozen professors as consultants in the areas of finance, biochemistry, and business management. With them, Elle has been working tirelessly to restructure my family's empire and transition us into clean energy by 2025. Of course, none of that will happen if we lose in court to my insane father, who is threatening to have his yoga cult take over.

*Totally. Bonkers.*

Even my mother is at a loss because while she's part owner, it's in name only. She gave my dad full executive authority years ago, which has become another piece of our messy court battle. Add to that, she's getting ready to divorce him. First things first though; we all agree the priority is containing my dad.

I ring the doorbell at my brother's place, a penthouse in downtown Houston that he uses on the weekends. During the week, while he's in school, he has an off-campus apartment.

The door opens, and I look up to see Henry's boyish smile and glowing green eyes, same color as mine.

"Is that my little Georgie? I almost didn't recognize you with the blonde hair." He lunges forward and captures me in a giant bear hug. "Love the new look."

I grunt, feeling a vertebra pop into place. "Ugh. Thanks. Now I can skip the chiropractor."

He sets me down. "Get your ass in here. Elle and I have some big news."

*Ohmygod.* They're pregnant. I just know it.

I walk inside the apartment that comes complete with floor-to-ceiling windows and a panoramic view of Houston. There's a terrace with a surround system, hot tub, and outdoor kitchen, where Elle is dancing to music as she flips burgers.

I set my purse on the marble breakfast bar overlooking the large chef's kitchen. "Okay. I'm ready. What's your news?"

Henry grins, and his smile is infectious. That's because he is as honest, sweet, and genuine as they come. It's no wonder he's fought my father's strongarm tactics since the day he was born. Henry never wanted to run the empire, and he made no secret about it. Now he's so close to achieving his dreams of the NFL that I can't help thinking he's my spirit animal of defiance. Plus, he sort of gets me, which is why I can be myself around him even if he treats me like a thing to be protected versus leaned on for support—an issue I've created and intend to rectify. After all, no one forced me to be shy.

"Okay," he says in that deep Henry voice. "We've done it."

"What?"

"We won."

I blink, attempting to decipher. "You mean against Dad?"

He nods. "A judge is signing the warrant to have Dad arrested as we speak. We found the copilot who refused to fly that day, and he will testify how Dad carefully planned your abduction and almost killed Claire in the process. There's enough evidence to convict him of kidnapping and attempted murder—four counts. They might even try to argue he's responsible for the death of the pilot, but that's a stretch."

My blood pressure tanks. *The pilot. Goddammit.* Why did Henry have to remind me? The man was never found, and I've spent every day since we returned to civilization trying to forget. No, I did not kill the pilot; however, I was the only one who saw him, and I turned my back. Me. No one else. I let him die, and my biggest regret is that I don't regret it enough. But any man who'd let a woman and her children die for a little cash doesn't deserve to live. Am I a bad person for feeling that way? I don't know.

"Wow. Dad's really going to jail?" I take a seat at Henry's breakfast bar, trying to breathe through my shock. My dad has so many people protecting him, I thought this day would never come.

"At least until the trial. Then he might end up in some mental institution, but who the fuck cares? He'll never hurt you guys again, and he sure as fuck won't ever control Walton Holdings. Now we just have to convince the court to keep us in charge."

As the heir, Henry was given temporary control while my father and the rest of us were missing, presumed dead. Now that we're all alive, we can't activate the will. Control has to be argued in court and then granted. Sadly, there are a lot of people out there filing disputes so they can be appointed trustees and do things their way, including giving themselves fat bonuses and raises, no doubt. When hundreds of billions of dollars are involved, people will do all sorts of things to get their hands on a piece.

"So…we still have to fight it out in court," I conclude.

"Yes," Henry replies. "Without hiccups. Not even a disruptive fart. It has to be business as usual."

This is so messed up. If our father died, my mother would get full control of their sixty percent ownership (we have forty percent). But since he's alive, the laws get all screwy, especially if the designated trustees are deemed incompetent. It has something to do with the oil companies being highly regulated and of public interest. Our lawyers even said that the court can order a liquidation of Walton Holdings and force us to auction off the companies since so many jobs and lives are at stake.

"But don't worry," Henry adds. "You'll be fine. I promised I'd always look after you. And I will."

I nod. "You're talking about money."

Frowning, he takes the stool next to me at the counter. "The money is for your future, Georgie, and I'm making sure you can do whatever you want with it—no strings attached—which is more than I ever got."

He's right. I know he is. And I'm grateful for this life I have. I won't ever starve. I won't ever go unloved. Yet I can't help wanting more. There's something sad and empty about living a life where I don't have the respect of the people I look up to most in this world. Not even after I saved my mother and sisters a few months ago. *Because you still act like you're lucky to eat the scraps from the table.* Maybe Abi is right. Brooks is the antidote to my illness. If I can endure him.

"Thank you, Henry." I muster a smile. "I don't know how I'll ever repay you and Elle for fighting for us."

He leans in, his eyes glossy with emotion. "Are you *fucking* joking me? I thought you were dead, Georgie. I thought I lost you all. If it weren't for Elle, I would've joined Dad in crazy town." He takes my right hand between his. "That phone call telling me you were alive was the miracle I'd been praying for."

I nod solemnly. "I'm sorry you went through all that."

"It doesn't matter now. You're safe. So are Mom, Claire, and Michelle. And I will never let anyone hurt you again, Georgie." He pulls me into his arms and hugs me tightly. "I'll keep you safe. Always."

I'm grateful for my big brother. More than words can say. But at the same time, I'm tired of being a fragile little mouse. I want to help my family and contribute, not be a burden. Especially at a time like this when things are such a mess.

"Henry!" bellows Elle, stepping inside with a plate of food. "Stop squeezing the life out of Georgie. She's turning blue."

He chuckles and lets go. "Like you this morning? So much blue. Or was that green?" he says to Elle.

"Hey!" she barks. "You weren't supposed to spill the baby beans until after dessert."

My jaw drops. "I'm going to be an auntie! I knew it." And I seriously feel like the news couldn't come at a better time. We all need something positive and wonderful to focus on. A baby will breathe new life into this family. *A fresh start for all of us.*

# CHAPTER SIX

It's Monday morning, my first day at work, as I'm tapping my freshly manicured fingernails on my desk just outside Nick Brooks's office. I have a company laptop, cell, and a temporary employee badge, which I bullshitted out of the hungover security guard at the front desk. If HR asks about my paperwork, I've got a complete list of excuses—*already submitted it online this morning. Check with IT. Oh, yeah. I made a mistake on the form and need to correct it. I'll bring it by later this week.* Honestly, I'm guessing I can make it three months before anyone catches on that I've yet to submit one piece of paperwork, provide my Social Security number, or have been paid; however, by my estimates, I only need a few weeks to show Henry, Michelle, and Claire that I can work just as hard as they can in a real company.

And what do I need to prove it? A glowing endorsement from Mr. Brooks.

*If only he'd show up.* I glance at my cell and note the time. 10:31 a.m. And all I've done is get him six coffees, which he hasn't drunk because he hasn't been to his office. But I found out from one of the sales assistants that he takes his coffee black, and I want to make a good impression. So every thirty minutes since I arrived, I've changed his cup, just hoping he'll come in and see how well I've attended to his needs.

*Come on. Come on.* I glance down the hallway for the hundredth time, hoping to hell that he'll step out of the elevator instead of a steady stream of my new coworkers, though they've been more than welcoming.

Jim, assistant sales manager for the West Coast, is only in town for the day, but very nice. I met Sarah, the data analyst for Brooks's team, who only crunches numbers for his direct reports because Brooks doesn't trust anyone to do the master forecast or sales roll-up. There were six other people who came by to say hi—I can't remember their names—but for the most part, everyone I've met this morning was helpful and pleasant. Oh, and they all chuckled as they wished me luck with Brooks. Needless to say, it's put me on edge, and I am two breaths away from passing out, running for the door, or finding a potted plant to hide behind until the building is empty.

The elevator down the hall chimes, and I lean forward over my desk for a clearer view. A woman steps out.

*Dammit.* I drop my head into my palms and

groan. "I'm in hell and the devil's missing."

"Nope. He's right here, coming from the stairwell after an all-morning meeting upstairs," says a deep, deep voice a few feet away.

I jerk up my head and find Mr. Brooks in a black suit and tie, staring down at me. For a brief moment, he seems *almost* pleased to see me—a subtle hunger in his light gray eyes. And the pleasant roll in my stomach *almost* makes me forget how horribly he treated me during the interview. Almost.

"Good morning," I say, my voice barely above a whisper.

His demeanor instantly shifts to something foul and acerbic. "Go get me some coffee, and don't let me hear talking again—not unless I ask you to speak."

My mouth sort of falls open. *What the hell is this man's problem?*

He disappears into his office, and it takes everything I have not to say something to him about women's rights. *Or people's rights.* The age of kings and serfdoms is long gone.

"Sonofabitch," I mutter to the coffee maker in the small break room on our floor. *He'd better shit golden eggs.*

I turn and head for his office, just one pucker away from spitting in his cup. When I get to his door, I hear him speaking quietly. "Yes. Yes, everything's on schedule. Just get off my back and let me do my job."

*Strange. I wonder what that's about.*

I knock loudly. "I h-have c-coffee." *Goddammit! Why can't I speak like a normal person?*

"Yes. Figures in by two o'clock. And don't be late," he bellows to whoever's on the phone.

I step inside with my java offering. "Your second cup, sir?" I say, barely able to speak above a whisper.

"I don't recall getting a first. And is there something the matter with your voice?"

"No-no."

"Then why are you whispering?"

*Use your big-girl voice, Georgie. Come on.* Instead I shrug and point like a moron to the window behind him at his first cup of coffee. "I tho-thought the sunlight would keep it warm."

He glances at the windowsill. "How the hell am I supposed to see it over there? Coffee goes on my desk."

I nod, set his cup down, and take two steps back like a timid little rabbit. I completely hate myself right now.

"And while we're talking protocols," he says, "I'd appreciate it if you wore something suitable to work. You represent me, and the last time I checked, I didn't shop in a dumpster."

Mortified, I look down at my clothes. I'm wearing a straight black skirt, brand new from Nordstrom. Claire never even wore it. My pink blouse has rhinestone buttons and a sash-style belt.

It's cute and professional. At least by my standards.

*I seriously can't believe the jerk just wardrobe shamed me.* I want to say something like, "*Back off, Miranda!*" But instead, out comes the word *yes.* Followed by my gaze falling to my feet in the classic submissive move. *Lift your eyes, you dipshit!* But my body doesn't obey.

"What was that?" He snarls with his silvery eyes. "I can't even hear you."

"I sa-said yes."

He looks at me, disgust written all over his full lips, which I know aren't used for loving or kissing. They're weapons of evil. "You're not brain damaged, are you?"

*What an asshole!* Yet I say nothing because I literally can't. My heart feels like it's going to implode with anger. My head is spinning.

"Oh, wonderful. I hired a mute idiot." He points toward the door. "Leave. I'll call if I need to be silently annoyed."

*You're a complete fucker. I hope you're hit by a bus.* I turn and head outside, closing the door behind me. I'm furious. And the sad part is that I'm more upset at myself for saying nothing.

I suddenly feel the tears welling in my eyes. I can't let him see me cry. Ohgod. No.

I speed walk to the ladies' room just next to the elevators, lock myself in a stall, and begin to bawl. *That man is a monster.* If it's the last thing I do, I will stand up to him.

"I'm so sorry I wasn't there to greet you on your first day," Abi says as I'm driving home in my black BMW Alpina. I'm not one for fancy cars, but my father never really gave me a choice. Maybe it's time to change that.

"Where were you? I seriously could've used a friend today."

"At some boring emergency off-site thing for Rebecca, but how'd it go?"

"My first day was magical," I tell her. "I learned where the coffee machine is. Oh, and the bathroom, where I spent most of the day crying."

"Oh no. What happened?"

"He basically called me stupid and told me I dress like a bag lady." I still can't believe it. "He's worse than my father."

"What? Seriously? Oh, Georgie, I'm so sorry."

"Why? I knew what I was getting into." Okay. Not really, but why make her feel bad? I came here willingly.

"Yeah, but I figured he just had a lot of man-tantrums and stole the credit for other people's work—your usual bad-boss moves. But if he really called you stupid, you can't let him get away with that." She sighs. "I'm so, so sorry."

"He actually called me a mute idiot," I clarify. "And don't be sorry. No one would ever believe that a human being could be so awful."

"Well, I'm going to see HR in the morning. He can't do that to my best friend."

"No," I protest. "I can't have them getting involved. In fact, the longer they go without knowing I exist, the better."

"But you can't just suck it up, Georgie."

"I won't. I'll stand my ground and slay the dragon—just like you said." But first, I'm going home, putting on my favorite red PJs, and burying my face in my teddy bear to muffle the sound of my hysterical sobs so my mother doesn't hear. Teddy and I go way, waaay back.

I hear Abi grumble on the other end of the line, and I know it's because she didn't anticipate this and feels like it's all her fault.

"I'll be fine," I say. "I mean it."

"Are you sure you don't want to quit?"

"I can't. Not after he treated me like that." If I walk away without standing up to him, I won't ever respect myself.

"Okay. Whatever you say, but I'm coming by for lunch tomorrow, and if he says one mean word, I can't guarantee I won't lose my shit."

She's a good friend. Really. But she needs her job, and I won't have her losing it on my account. "Better we meet down in the lobby. And if I'm not there around noon, I'll be in the women's bathroom crying again."

# CHAPTER SEVEN

*Approximately Four Months Ago.*

Michelle and I have been locked in a cement hut for over a week now. No sign of my mother or Claire. The only thing we know is that we are near the ocean, either some remote beach or on an island. Oh, and apparently, the people here do not wear clothes, but that's not the worst of it.

Once a day, two women and an armed man visit us in their birthday suits to deliver fresh water and basic foods: mangos, bananas, and dry fish.

Wait. It's weirder.

In order to get the food, we are forced to do thirty minutes of yoga poses on the dirt floor.

"Your mind cannot be healthy if your body is not sound," the man said on our first day.

"Fuck you," Michelle had replied back. "I'm not the one holding people against their will and letting her junk hang out. By the way, have any of you ever heard of a razor? Because those tumbleweeds on your crotches are just nasty."

"No yoga. No food," the man had growled.

Ever since then, it's been a battle of wills, which always ends with us doing the sun salute or some fucked-up tree pose. Clothed, of course. And when we ask what's happened to the rest of our family, they simply smile and bow their heads. "*Namaste.*"

"I swear," says Michelle after having just completed today's round of fitness torture, "if we ever get out of here, I'm doing everything in my power to make yoga illegal."

"But did you see the abs on that woman?" I say. "She must live off nothing but tofu."

"I'd like to choke her with it. I mean, what the hell do they think will come of helping Dad with his insane plot?"

Poor Michelle. I know she misses her husband, Chukwuemeka. She met him while on a business trip to Nigeria, and they haven't been apart since. It's sweet, really. I just know I'll never have that kind of love with a man. Every guy I've ever met wants to take care of me, which I hate, so that means I'll be single forever. *Especially if we don't get off this island.*

"I just wish I knew why Dad was doing this," I say.

"You heard Mom on the plane. He's finally lost it."

"But he didn't show any signs of insanity leading up to this." Quite the opposite. He was calm and cool during the crash, like everything was playing out according to plan.

"No signs?" Michelle scoffs. "For the last two years, he's been doing naked yoga in his office at 11:00 a.m."

"True. But what if it's all part of a plan?" My father is cold and calculating. He's always thinking one hundred steps ahead.

"Doubtful. And it doesn't change the facts: We're locked in here, and he almost killed Claire, not to mention us. I don't care what motives he has; the man has a screw loose."

"Agreed." But while Michelle has been spending her time stewing these past few days, I've been keeping my eyes and ears open. I know the ocean is directly to the west because I can hear the waves when the wind blows just right. I can see the sun rising in the morning through a narrow crack in the cement wall. I know that we can't possibly be far from the mainland US because we were flying east out of Houston for four hours. I know because I had the window shade up the entire flight, and had we been traveling south, I would have had to close it since the sun would have been west and shining right on my laptop screen. Plus, my dad is no fool. He knows like I do that entering into another country's airspace, say Mexico or Cuba—the only countries within a four-hour reach from Houston— would require us to file additional paperwork and another flight plan. No, he wanted to keep it simple and make it look like we vanished into thin air.

*We're in the Florida Keys or on a private island nearby.* That's my guess, anyway. And if I'm right, it won't be too hard for us to get away.

# CHAPTER EIGHT

*Present Day.*

It's day two working for the Antichrist, and I've spent the entire morning mentally preparing my speech, which will set the ground rules: "*Mr. Brooks, first, I want you to know how excited I am to work for you because I've heard you're a genius and I am here to learn. Second, I'm willing to work hard and stay late doing whatever you need of me, and you won't hear me complain about it either. Third, but most important, you need to know that I will not tolerate being spoken to like a piece of dirt. You are not to comment on my clothes, my body or looks, or on my intelligence. It's hurtful and wrong.*" I'm banking on the fact that he has a soul hidden somewhere deep inside and can't really feel good about being such a dick to people. Plus, there were the looks he gave me. Was I wrong when I sensed something between us?

*More like crazy or delusional.* I could never have a connection with a man like him. He's horrible, and I'm going to tell him so.

Sitting at my desk, I get out my compact to give myself a little nonverbal encouragement. *You got this, girl!*

"I know you're not sitting there doing your makeup like a tenth grader," says that voice I've come to loathe in world-record time.

*Oh no. Brooks.* Obviously, he thinks he's caught me primping like some vain airhead. I drop my compact and feel my body tighten up in some weird flight-or-fight response reserved for life-or-death danger.

*No. No. I can do this. I can set him straight.* I lift my chin to tell him that we must talk. Immediately. In his office. I can even hear my voice inside my head saying the words with a tone that's "all business, buster!" But when I open my mouth, the self-esteem-gobbling gremlin reaches in and snatches away my words. *Holy shit balls! Really?*

Brooks stares down at me with those soulless pale eyes, his silky dark brows knitted together. "You know, Gail, I planned on firing you first thing this morning. I figured, what's a guy like me going to do with a dumpster in a skirt who can't even speak." He leans down, placing us almost nose to nose. "But you know what?" he whispers, the disdain in his voice oozing from every syllable. "I think I'm going to keep you around."

"Wha-why?" He clearly hates me, though I'm unsure what I did to deserve it.

He stares for a long moment and suddenly licks

his lips. And screw me, but the way he's looking at me doesn't feel like hate anymore.

He jerks upright and straightens his tie. "Because it's actually therapeutic to tell you how pathetic you are. You're so unnoticeable that I can look at your face and imagine any loser who's managed to piss me off. Now get me some coffee, Gail. And then book me a flight to New York for tomorrow morning. I'll return next Wednesday evening."

*What the fuck is the matter with this guy?* On the inside, I'm in a rage. But on the outside, I know I'm sitting there looking like a worthless fool about to break into tears. Honestly, I'm crying already. He just can't see it. I'm ashamed of myself because I know I deserve to be treated like a human being with feelings. I'm a good person. I care about other people. So why, dammit? Why the fuck won't I open my mouth? I might be shy, but I can still say no. I can say stop. I can say how horrible he his. Standing up for one's self doesn't require being verbose.

I lift my chin and rise from my desk, certain that this is the moment. My moment. But when I notice him waiting expectantly, like he's itching for me to wow him with a bit of claws and teeth, I buckle.

"What's that?" He bends down, cupping his hand to his hear. "Couldn't hear you, dumpster girl."

*Oh no. Oh no. Don't, Georgie. Please...*But my plea falls on my own deaf ears. Before I know it, this evil, deceivingly beautiful man is witnessing a warm tear trickle down my cheek.

He shakes his head. "Goddamn, you're pitiful. Let's do us both a favor, sweetheart. You stay home where you belong, crying to your mamma, who I'm sure is just as delightfully trashy-looking as you, and I'll forget I ever hired you." He turns and heads into his office. "Don't forget to book my flight before you go." He slams the door, and I run to the ladies' room to sob.

"Sydney? You in here?" Right around noon, Abi's voice is outside the stall where I've been sitting for the last hour contemplating the nature of my failure. I'm furious at myself. Furious! But of course, that only leads to more tears.

I sniffle in response.

"Oh, honey..." Her voice is sadder than I've ever heard, and I know what she's thinking. She wants to save me. She wants to protect me from that epic dickhead, but she can't. Even if she could, it's not what I want. Imagine that your biggest dream in the universe is to play Rachmaninoff on the piano and to play it to perfection. Standing ovation. Packed music hall. Now imagine your best friend pats you on the back and tells you to stand beside her while she plays for you because you can't figure out how to do it on your own. That's not a dream fulfilled. It's a dream that's fizzled in the worst way possible.

"Just go, Abi," I whimper. "I can't take you feeling sorry for me. I do that well enough on my own."

*What an idiot I am!* I'd actually thought Brooks might have an ounce of humanity inside him. And those looks he gave me? He was probably thinking about how much fun he'd have watching me cry. *Jerkface!*

"Really, I'll be fine. Just go," I sputter.

The silence on the other side of the stall door is palpable. "Okay, Syd. Call me later?"

"Yeah. I'll call."

Her heels click across the tile floor, and I hear the door squeak open and shut.

I cover my face with my hands and let out one last juicy sob. *I hate him. I hate him. I hate him!* And I know I have it in me to fight back, but something's holding me back. *Okay, Georgie. Where's the girl who fought for her sisters and mother on that beach?*

Suddenly, I'm thinking about that pilot again and the way I so coldly turned my back. It was so unlike me, yet I did it. I could easily see myself doing it again, too, because the rage I felt is still there. *The audacity of that man to threaten me and my family.* Regardless, knowing I have it in me to be so vindictive and heartless is truly unsettling.

*Shit. Maybe that's the problem.* My fear, at least part of it, could be the fact that I don't want to end up like my father, because I can't deny that the piece of me I'm suppressing isn't a saint. *Dear God. I'm a closet asshole.* Chester Walton's daughter. If I let her out, I might become everything I hate.

*For fuck's sake, Georgie. Now you're just being delusional. Listen to yourself!* I am nothing like that dick-tator. Not even on my worst day. I am kind and gentle, but fiercely loyal. I am quiet, resourceful, and smart.

*I am a warrior squirrel.* Yes. That's what I am. And warrior squirrels don't carry swords. We move silently like the wind. We sneak to get what we want. But most of all, we crack nuts. And Brooks, if anything, is surely one of those.

I have been going about this the wrong way, trying to make myself into something I'm not, instead of using what I've got to my advantage.

*And now I know what I must do.* I'm going to get him fired.

# CHAPTER NINE

Imagine, if you will, a stormy sky and you're that little warrior squirrel standing on a rock in a dry riverbed. Off in the distance, you hear rain and see the black clouds unleashing their fury. While you're standing there, watching with equal measures of fear and awe, a wall of water rushes toward you. You have one second to decide: Run your furry little ass off, or dig those claws into the rock and hope for the best.

Knowing how fast squirrels are, most of us would choose to run. But I am a warrior squirrel and have decided to face the storm head-on. Which is why I've spent the entire past week and weekend focusing on two things: studying for my makeup finals for last semester and making Brooks's life hell with a carefully planned mindfuck. *I'm going to wreck this man.* Yes, revenge is part of it, but a tiny piece of me wants his respect too. Not that I care what he thinks. Okay, okay. I do care, but only because I want him to feel a little pain when he realizes he's messed with the wrong woman.

I release a breath, pick up the phone on my desk, and dial Travel. I haven't seen Brooks since the middle of last week, and it's now Wednesday, so he's due back from New York tonight.

"Meg speaking," says the woman on the phone.

"Hi, Meg. This is Geor—" *Crap! That was close.* "This is…Geographic National's biggest travel lover, Sydney Lucas, Mr. Brooks's new intern."

"Errrr…thank you for that tidbit of useless info. And don't you mean *National Geographic*?"

I wince. "Yep. But you know us travelin' types and our nicknames: Geo Nat. Nat Geo. We roll loose and free, yanno?" *I'm an idiot.*

"I have no clue what you're saying, but what can I do for you, Geo Nat Sydney, the intern weirdo?"

*Ugh. Fuck her.* "I booked Mr. Brooks on an RT to NYC last week. He's there now but says he's staying oh-forty-eight hours past zero. Copy."

"Are you high? No, really. I get that the ganja is legal in some states, but showing up to work high is illegal everywhere."

*Dammit.* I'm freaking out and my brain is misfiring my mouth. "Sorry. It's my…military upbringing." I wince. There's not a person on this planet in the military who acts this lame.

"Sure. Whatever. So when does Brooks want to return to Houston?"

*Shit. Shit.* I hadn't thought of that. My plan only went as far as stranding him in New York. "He said he wasn't sure and to leave it open until further notice."

I hear the clicking of her fingertips on the other end of the phone. "Oh…kay! He's all set. I'm sending the revised itinerary—"

"Ju-just send it t-to me. He said his email is down and asked me to text it to him."

I wait with bated breath.

"Sure," she says.

*Yes!* She bought it. The best part is that I heard one of the managers in the bathroom talking to a coworker about the travel department being short-handed for the next two weeks since Meg will be on vacation. Brooks won't be able to ask her who altered his flight. And when he tries to call me from the road, he'll find his cell has been reported missing and no longer functions. He'll be left trying to borrow a phone at the airport—*good luck with that!*—and like most people, he's not likely to have any work numbers memorized. He'll eventually get the main PVP number, but nobody answers past four. He's going to be SOL stuck at JFK. If he tries to book a flight on his own, well, I have a few other surprises for him. *Like, uh-oh! Someone reported your company credit card as lost and it's no longer active!*

Who would do such a horrible thing? *Warrior squirrel.*

"Thank you, Meg," I say in my usual quiet voice. "I'll call back as soon as I have his return info. Oh, and have a really awesome vacation."

"Thanks, ganja Syd."

She ends the call, and I let out a long breath. Great. I'm now pothead Syd. If the reward of my retaliation weren't so great, I'd be mortified. But the nectar of victory is waiting. *So sweet.*

With phase one complete, I go to the next step—getting him fired—and log in to Mr. Brooks's personal secure server. He's giving a presentation this afternoon in New York to a bunch of physicians from some of the top hospitals across the country. It's a big deal because getting them to prescribe our drugs is how we make money, and I hear that funding our cutting-edge R & D is very expensive. No, I don't want to sabotage the company, so I will make it look like human error. One human in particular. We'll make it up to the doctors with fruit baskets and free golf clubs or something.

I open Brooks's presentation and grin. He only works off the server in case his laptop crashes or gets lost. The bonehead doesn't even keep a backup on a flash drive. But why would he? Our servers are *sooo* safe.

I begin toggling through the slides, making subtle changes. "*Efficacy rate among patients is over forty percent.*"

*You are now…*

"*Mortality rate among patience is eighty percent…*" I hear Brooks's "patience" dying already.

Next, I swap out his graph—showing the long-term cost comparison of our drugs versus the competition—with a graph I found that compares the growth of online porn to a surge in bestiality.

*Oh, and look! Let's add a caption for the doctors underneath that graph: "Nine out of ten doctors prescribe sheep for Nick Brooks. Because he's a sadistic wanker."*

*Is that too much?* I wonder. *Nah!* Not like he's even going to suspect me because no one but him has access to his server.

So how'd I get in? Well, remember Robbie, the tech geek who makes fake driver's licenses? For a hundred bucks, he'll hack into anything. Including, oh yes, bank accounts. Which for Brooks now has a whopping $0 balance.

*Uh-oh. Looks like your checks are going to bounce.* I smile with a contented sigh. He'll get the money back in a week, but once these doctors complain about Brooks, he'll be one step out the door. These are major clients, and I doubt our president is going to ignore them. Best of all, he'll know someone is messing with his life, and timid little Sydney—oh so helpless—is the last person he'll suspect. I mean, I can't even dress myself properly, right?

With his cell not working, his presentation sabotaged, his money gone and flight cancelled, it's time to get to work on his office. I've got one more thing planned, but it must wait until he returns from New York.

"Whenever that is." I smile. "Never mess with a smart woman, Nick."

꙰ ꙰

Friday morning, I am sitting at my desk when the boogeyman slithers in. "Good morning, Mr. Brooks. How was your shitty long trip? I've packed up your office," I say with a smug smile.

Okay. That's only what happens in my mind. Really, I'm sitting at my desk, typing up an email for Rebecca, Abi's boss. I bumped into her in the morning and mentioned that Brooks hadn't given me anything to do. She hopped right on the opportunity for extra help, so now I'm happily busy and giddy with delight. *I can't wait to see Brooks's tattered expression when he finally makes it home.*

But when Brooks walks in just past eleven, his beautiful face is clean shaved. His corpse-gray eyes are bright and twinkling, like he had a good night's rest, and his black suit, which fits his tall masculine frame like a glove, is freshly pressed.

My heart does a little pitter-patter. *What the... You are not pittering or pattering for that man just because he looks so good.* Especially given that his glowing mood means my plan has gone terribly wrong. He should be a pissy mess!

"You still here?" he snarls.

"Yes." I nod dumbly.

"Then get me some coffee." He enters his office, and I'm doing my best to hide my shock.

*How did my plan not work?* Okay. He's not stupid. Maybe he caught the mistakes before he gave his presentation. And maybe he just used a personal credit card to fly home. I mean, I couldn't shut down all of his access to money.

*All right. Regroup, Georgie. Regroup.* I open his calendar and see he has a meeting with our president, Mr. Craigson, in five minutes.

*Wow. Okay. Maybe Craigson is coming to fire him.* My plan might've worked and Brooks is just playing it cool.

I'm unsure, but this is perfect! I've got a little career-wrecking surprise waiting for Brooks inside and—*Wait. Wait. What if I make sure Craigson gets to witness Brooks's awesome leadership skills?* If Craigson is coming down here, I can give him a second reason to fire the a-hole.

I wait patiently until I spot Craigson step off the elevator. To my delight, he actually stops to chat with some guy in a cubicle. This is wonderful.

I get up and knock on Brooks's door.

"Come in," his deep voice calls out.

I open the door, step inside, and shut it for one very good reason. I want him to feel comfortable yelling at me.

"Oh, it's you." He frowns and goes back to working on his laptop. "What do you want, Cindy?"

First I'm Gail. Now I'm Cindy? *Okay.* I stand there wanting to say something that will push him through the roof like, *"You're a stupid creep and I've learned absolutely nothing from you."* But of course, my mouth and brain are never in sync.

"Well?" he prods impatiently.

"I, uh…"

"Dear God, woman, spit it out or leave. I have things to do, none of which you're qualified to assist with, given they require a functioning brain. Did your mother smoke and drink while pregnant with you, or did she just hit the crack pipe?"

*Ohmygod! He insulted my mother! Again!* I feel the rage build, and I'm unsure if it's because he's picked on someone I love or because his words are particularly mean this time.

"Well? Which is it?" he prods. "Because I know there has to be a reason for that thick, inbred look on your dumb face. And didn't I tell you to stop stealing clothes from the homeless?"

*Asshole!* This man has got to go—from this company, from my life, from this planet!

"Why are you so fucking cruel!" I belt out to my complete and utter shock. Then, all of a sudden, words are flowing from my mouth, and I want to sing and dance (on Brooks's fat handsome head) and never stop. "You are the most vile, condescending, despicable man I have ever met. No. Wait. You're not a man; you're less than human. You're a pig! A goddamned shit-covered pig. I mean, where do you get off calling me names and swinging your dick around like we're all supposed to suck it just because you can sell stuff? Well, fuck you, Brooks! Swing your big dick at some other woman, because I'm smart. And I'm kind. And my clothes are perfectly fine you...*asshole*!"

A smug smile creeps over his full lips as he leans back in his chair and folds his arms over his broad chest. "Well, looks like you *do* have it in you. Very good, Cindy. But next time you'd like to talk about my big dick, how about doing it out of earshot of Mr. Craigson there?"

My feet meld with the gray carpeted floor. *Oh, dammit. He's standing right behind me, isn't he?* I slowly turn to see Craigson's white hair and cold blue eyes. I've actually met him once at our Thanksgiving charity event last year, but I'm sure he wouldn't remember me. I hid in my room most of the time. Plus, I have a new hair color.

Mr. Craigson clears his throat. "I see your fan club is growing by leaps and bounds, Brooks." He walks past me and takes a seat in front of the desk. I'm mortified, but he doesn't seem to give a crap about my outburst.

"Yeah, well," Brooks leans forward in his chair, "I'm here to make obscene amounts of money, not friends. And they're here to work, not bitch and complain like pussies."

"Well, keep up the good work. We couldn't be happier," Craigson says.

*Huuuh?* It seems that none of my plans worked. *The man is actually getting praise!*

Brooks looks at me, and there's a hint of pride on those lips. "Let's catch up later, sweetheart." He winks.

*What is happening?* Like a stiff board, I swivel my rigid body and leave, closing the door behind me. *Oh my God. Did he just wink at me, all Mr. Charming like, as if to say, "Hey, Cindy, way to go, woman?" He totally did.*

I suddenly can't help but wonder if he's been pushing my buttons on purpose. *A test?*

*No. He's a giant jerk, and he needs to go!*

I sit in my chair, grab my phone, and stare at the playlist. This is my last move. If Craigson doesn't fire Brooks for this, nothing will work. I hit play.

Suddenly, the sound of a man saying, "Suck it, baby. Suck it hard!" followed by a woman orgasming booms through the office from underneath my desk.

*What the…?* I look and the Bluetooth speaker I hid in Brooks's office is sitting at my feet with a note.

*Nice try, sweetheart.*

—*N.B.*

I scramble to shut it off and cover my mouth. He must've either gotten into the office before me, or he came in last night. But how did he know to look for it?

*Wait. Who cares? I stood up for myself! I finally did it!* Curse words and everything. I just took a monumental step, and this is a moment to be proud of!

"Porn at work?" says a woman walking by my desk, shaking her head.

"Oops! Sorry. My laptop caught a virus." *And I've just caught an epic case of confidence.*

# CHAPTER TEN

"If only I'd thought of that!" Abi says as we walk out of the building and head through the underground parking garage to grab her car and go to lunch. My car is parked three blocks away since it cost about one hundred and fifty thousand dollars. Not your usual intern car.

Abi goes on, "Really, I'm so proud of you for yelling at him."

"I'm proud, too."

"So now what?" she asks.

"Well, now I need him to let me do some serious work—a big project with a presentation."

"You think he'll let you just because you yelled at him one time?"

It's a valid question. "I'm hoping he will. Not like I've got months to earn his respect. My family needs help now-now." Also, if I stay too long, I'll be found out.

"All right. Let's assume he says yes. Do you think you're ready to stand up in front of a room full of people and give an actual presentation? Not that I think you can't. I just know you'll need time to work up to it."

She's right, as usual, which means I need to step up the pace in my "occupational therapy." Just then, we walk by a really nice-looking Harley, electric blue and sleek chrome. My father has a few bikes, and I know they're not cheap, but this one is especially expensive. It has custom blue stitching and extra-large tires.

"It's Brooks's," Abi says.

"Really now." I start digging through my purse for a pen.

"What do you think you're doing?"

"Continuing my training. Keep an eye out, wudja?" I crouch beside the bike and start letting the air out of the back tire.

"Oh my God, Georgie. Seriously?" Her head whips from side to side. "Hurry. We're going to get caught."

"No. We're not. That's why you're keeping a lookout."

She groans, but does like a good friend, giving me a few precious minutes to deflate half the tire. Brooks might know it's me, but he's got it coming. *Wait.* Does he know I'm behind the bank hacking, too?

*No way.* A porn soundtrack and a flat tire do not a hacker make.

"I don't see how that's going to help you," she says. "Messing with a man's Harley might be crossing the line."

"Or it might make him fear me. Just a little." With my task complete, Abi and I nonchalantly stroll to her car and leave. "Lunch is on me," I say with a grin.

We get into her blue Jetta, and she turns to me with tight lips and a frown. "Georgie, can I ask you something?"

"Sure."

"What's your game plan after all this?"

"What do you mean?" I ask.

"Well, if you're successful and prove you can hold your own in this type of environment, what are you planning to do?"

"Work. Help my family. Finish school next year." I came back from yoga hell too late to register for this semester, but I'll go back in the fall. I still have to take my makeup finals for last December, though. I'm waiting for the university's board to give the approval. My circumstances were extenuating, and I wasn't really in the frame of mind to take the finals the moment I got back, which means I missed the makeup window. I'm ready now, however. I've been slowly reading my materials and preparing over the last month. Still, I've got between now and August with nothing to do but help my family. If I end up taking a job, like at one of our green tech companies, I can delay school another semester if I have to. Whatever's needed.

"But you do realize you'll have to make sure

Brooks is fired eventually, right?" she says. "I mean, whether or not he helped you in his own twisted way, he can't treat people like that. It's wrong, not to mention it's only a matter of time before someone sues and PVP is held liable for letting him go unchecked."

I blink. It's something I hadn't thought of, because up until now, it's been all about helping my family through this tough situation and trying to survive a terminal case of shyness. But she's right. I own part of PVP—at least my family trust does, which is part mine. That makes me an owner. Also, my brother, Henry, is the acting CEO of our holdings company and technically has direct oversight of PVP. I have an obligation to have Brooks removed, which was my intent, only now, something is urging me to stick with him. *That would be my insanity.*

"The last thing we all need right now is a scandal. That's for sure," I think out loud. "I'll have to do something about him after I'm done."

Besides, for the time being I can see that Craigson doesn't give a rat's patootie about Brooks's behavior as long as the sales keep pouring in. I will have to deal with them both another way and act when the time is right, but I will act. For the moment, we're fighting too many battles, and we can't afford another.

෨ ෧

When I return from lunch, there's a note on my desk from Brooks to come see him. My heart starts to pound in my chest, and I feel the familiar burning of stomach acid.

*No, Georgie. You're done with that.* I'm not, of course, but I have to start pushing myself to believe it.

I go to his door and knock lightly.

"Come in," says the deep growl of a voice.

Resisting my instincts to run, I peek my head through the crack. "You wanted to see me?" My voice is quiet, but it's clear and stutter-free. A monumental step in the right direction.

"Take a seat. We need to talk." He sounds angry, and it's scary. Especially since I know he's about to chew me out for the incident from earlier.

I walk over, avoiding eye contact until I'm seated. I draw a deep breath and then slowly bring my eyes to his. His lips are relaxed, the bottom one slightly fuller than the top, making his mouth seem less like a weapon of war and more like a tool of seduction. Not that I would ever in a million years consider him a man worth being seduced by. However, I'll admit that he's unjustly good looking, clearly works out—takes lots of manly muscles to stretch a suit like that—and that he's the kind of guy a woman would stop to look at on the street. But the anger, the cruelty, the unchivalrous attitude make it impossible for me to appreciate how good looking he his.

*Only you just appreciated it.*

*Oh. Stop it.*

"Well? Do you have anything to say?" he asks.

"Ummm…no. Not really." Again, I speak quietly, but at least I'm speaking.

"No apology for all of the dick-swinging comments and insults?"

*You deserved every word.* I shake my head no.

A sly smile creeps across his lips. It's then I notice how the two hollows of his cheeks actually pucker into boyish dimples when he smiles.

*Ugh.* I frown. *Where the hell does this guy get off having boyishly cute anything?*

"I'm glad," he says. "You should never apologize when you're in the right."

"Are you sa-saying," *dammit! No stutters*, "that you're happy about what I said?"

"Frankly, I was ready to have you tossed out on your ass if you didn't stand up for yourself."

I'm blown away. He can't possibly mean what I think. "So it *was* a test? And you're not really an asshole?"

"Oh, I'm definitely an asshole. But anyone who wants to work for me has to be immune to it or they have no place here. Sales is the toughest role at any company, whether you're selling ad space or vacuum cleaners. You have to have balls, and you can't fear rejection. So if you're ready to check the timid-mouse act at the door and open that little mouth of yours to form actual words, I have some work for you."

I'm in shock. All his bullshit nastiness was really the Nick Brooks Sales Boot Camp? Not that his confession in any way, shape, or form excuses his behavior. However, what shocks me most is that he now seems interested in letting me do some real work.

"What's the project?" I squeak. "I mean," I lower my voice, "what's the project?"

"I've got a small presentation I need to throw together for a six o'clock meeting. I need some data pulled and thrown into a spreadsheet along with one summary slide. Think you can handle it?"

"Yes."

"Great. I'll email the details now." Brooks looks at his watch.

*That's funny.* It's a cheap Rolex knockoff. I know this because Michelle bought one for Chewy by accident off some website. When he took it into a jewelry store to size it, they told him it was a fake. They don't sell the orange face with the gold and silver band. It only comes in solid silver. Brooks's watch has two kinds of metal.

*Hmmm…I wonder if he knows?* Likely not, because a man who makes his kind of salary would never wear a fake.

"All right," he says. "Well, get to work. Mr. Walton said he might stop by early if he can."

*Walton?* My back goes ramrod straight. "Sorry?"

"Henry Walton. He's the son of Chester Walton. Craigson asked me to step in since he's got some FDA regulatory thing to deal with."

"Wa-Walton?" I gulp.

"Please don't tell me you haven't heard of them?"

I pucker my lips. "Nope. Can't say that I have."

"They own the company? Their names are splashed all over the news because the family is trying to oust the father?"

"Oh. *Those* Waltons." I shrug. "I thought you meant that old TV show or something."

He frowns, likely wondering if I'm dumber than he thought. "Just have it all ready by four so I have time to look it over."

I turn, eager to leave because I'm already thinking that all is not lost. Brooks didn't say I needed to stick around for the meeting. That means I can give him the data and get the hell out of here before Henry sees me.

"Oh, and, Sally," Brooks says, "you'll have to stay late for the meeting. Just in case Henry Walton has any additional requests."

*Crap.* I nod stiffly. "Of course, Mr. Brooks."

What the hell am I going to do?

# CHAPTER ELEVEN

*Approximately Two and a Half Months Ago.*

We've been held prisoner now for almost eight weeks. Christmas, New Year's, and my birthday have come and gone without any sign of their existence with the exception of the hugs we shared. Claire is with us now and has recovered nicely, though they had to shave part of her hair off when they did the stitches. She says she didn't see much of my mother during the weeks she was in recovery, but that Mom did attempt to escape and come find us. Sadly, my mother was caught, and now she's locked up somewhere on this island. Or remote beach. Or wherever we are.

But tonight, we're making our move. I've been paying careful attention, and for the last two weeks, no one has been outside our hut around eleven fifteen at night. The guy leaves and another arrives about five minutes after. I've tested it six times, calling for the guard. No one replies during that window. I've also overheard them speaking about my mother not being too far away, making references like: "Hey, can you get Georgina more water?" The reply being: "I'll go next door in a sec."

Claire can see I'm nervous and grabs my hand. "It's okay, Georgie. They're not going to hurt us. If that was their goal, they would've done it by now."

"I don't think they'd harm us intentionally, but something could go wrong," I say.

"Don't think that way," says Michelle. "Just stay calm and focus that big brain of yours, okay? You need to make sure we head in the right direction after we get Mom."

I know I'm the one who figured out the logistics of our escape plan, but that doesn't mean I'm brave like my sisters.

Claire looks at her watch. "Everyone ready?"

Michelle and I nod.

"On the count of three, we kick. One, two, *three*!" Claire yells.

We slam the soles of our bare feet against the wooden door. Whatever's got us bolted in isn't strong. I can already see the doorjamb buckling.

"Hurry! Harder!" Claire yells.

The door busts open, exposing what looks to be dark jungle ahead. We rush out and immediately see five more grass roof huts like ours and a dimly lit walkway going off to our left.

"I'll take this hut." I point to the closest structure. Michele and Claire go to the others at the far end.

"Mom?" No one answers in the first structure, so I go to the next hut. "Mom!" I whisper loudly. "Mom!"

"Georgie?" Her voice is muted through the rickety door, but I know it's her.

"Guys! She's here." I slide the bolt on the outside, and my mother rushes out, wrapping her arms around me.

"Oh, thank God you're okay." She squeezes so hard I can't breathe, but I couldn't care less.

Michelle and Claire run to us and give a quick hug to my mother because there's no time for a sniffly reunion.

"Come on, we need to run!" I point directly west, and the four of us head into the night, praying to God that this is the end of our nightmare.

Little do we know, it's just the beginning of the horror, and the things I will see tonight cannot be unseen or forgotten. Giant. Hairy. Balls.

# CHAPTER TWELVE

*Present Day.*

It's four thirty, and I am a dizzy, stressed-out mess. Brooks just called me into his office to review my work while at the same time informing me that Henry will indeed arrive early. At any moment, my brother is going to step from that elevator, see me, and go ballistic because I lied about my name and put our family in the crosshairs of scandal.

But I have a plan.

This warrior squirrel is going to run like the wind. Brooks will think I've lost my nerve, for which I will pay dearly; however, that is a far more savory option.

I hit *Send* on my email to Brooks so he has the best and final numbers, which I've triple-checked. I grab my purse and make a mad dash for the back stairwell.

"Where are you going, Gail?" says that baritone voice.

*I'm Gail again?* I freeze with my back to him.

"Errr…bathroom."

"Ladies' room is the other way." He points over his shoulder toward the elevator bank.

I squeeze my eyes shut for a moment. *Think. Think.* "That one's dirty. All covered in diarrhea." *Oh, Jesus. How gross.*

The corners of his godlike lips turn down in disappointment. "Or maybe you're trying to sneak out before Henry Walton shows up."

*Crapola.* I crinkle my nose. I know I'm caught, which still leaves the option of running but makes it far less dignified.

I turn, praying he might take pity on me, and shrug. "Guilty as charged?" My words come out like a ten-year-old elf's. Tiny, squeaky, high-pitched.

He crosses those noticeably fit arms over his noticeably fit chest. His coat is off, red tie loose, and his white dress shirt is unbuttoned to his collarbone. His sleeves are rolled up to the elbows, so I can see the ropes of muscle on his forearms. Low and behold, there's a tattoo with USMC in vertical block letters on his right arm.

*I knew it.* His tough demeanor, strong body, and confident stance instantly made me think Marines when we first met. It explains why he hates weakness. I hear they practically beat it out of them in the Corps. Ironically, it only makes him more human to me.

He notices me looking and unrolls his sleeve. "I served in the Middle East," he says. "And I don't discuss it."

"Oh. Okay," I say quietly. "I won't ever ask."

"Good. Now get your ass in my office. We have a meeting to prepare for, and it's an important one."

Despite my state, my curiosity is piqued. Why is Henry here to see Brooks? "What's the purpose of the meeting?"

"Henry Walton is impressed with my sales team and is considering having me take over some of the other companies. He hopes we can adapt what I've done here."

"Oh." Of course, this would be Elle's idea since she's the brains behind the operations. Not that Henry isn't smart because he is. It's just that he's focused on finals, the NFL, and helping Elle at a consultative level. He's the face; she's the brains.

*Ugh. But Brooks?* Expanding into our other companies? This is not good. He might know his stuff and have killer instincts, but he is not the kind of man we need running—I mean ruining—things. Example being, he just told me to get my "ass" in his office.

"Well, con-congrats?" I say sheepishly.

"Not yet." He points to his office, indicating that he's still waiting for my *ass* to get a move on.

I blow out a flubbery sound and march inside. This is it. The end of my escapade. But I can't continue regardless. I'll have to come clean with Henry because we won't want an asshole like Nick Brooks at the helm of sales.

Brooks grabs one of the chairs in front of his desk and drags it around to his side. "Come and sit, Candy."

"Sydney," I correct, feeling ridiculous. It's not even my real name, and in a matter of minutes, he'll know I am Georgie Walton, named after my mother, Georgina, Texan royalty whose great grandfather was the first to discover oil in our great state in 1903.

"Sydney." He winks and flashes that smile again. It's devilish and charming and…

*He knew my name was Sydney all along.* It was just one more way to push my buttons. I'd be pissed, but I'm far too freaking nervous about the impending drama with my brother.

Brooks takes a seat while I remain standing. "Come on, Sydney. I don't bite."

I narrow my eyes at him.

"Fine. I do. But I'll behave just for you." He pats the chair beside him, and I come around. I don't know why I'm complying, since this ruse is about to implode.

Immediately, he begins going over the file I sent and points to the screen. "Ah, you see there. You never want to give the best news first when you're making a pitch. You start with the bad news, the challenges, the failures. Make them think you're going to tell them the most tragic story they've ever heard."

I sit and lean in toward the screen. "Why?"

"Pretend you own a used-car lot. The sales manager, who has a monthly goal of three hundred car sales, walks in and tells you she sold five hundred this month."

I like that he said "she." He doesn't assume the manager is a guy.

"Okay," I say.

"Now imagine that following this news of five hundred cars, which is quite good, she tells you she could've done better, but they didn't close half of the sales because the customers walked away. Now how do you feel about her exciting news?"

I give it some thought. "I guess I'm still happy, but—"

"But the shine is tarnished. She failed to do the one thing most sales people fail at: to sell their successes. Now imagine that same manager comes in and says: 'Well, I have bad news, boss. Half the customers walked away before we could close.' Now, how are you feeling about her work?" he asks.

"Not good."

"Right." Brooks points to the numbers on the screen. "But then she shows the results. You see that she's pulled off a miracle because despite the hurdles, she gave you much more than you asked for."

I process that for a moment. "But what happens if you don't exceed targets?"

"It happens. Sure. But even then you always start with the bad news. People are more grateful when they think it's doomsday and you give them some good news."

"So when you show this to my b—" *Dammit.* I was about to say *my brother.* "To our boss's boss, you want him to see the dropped accounts, the declining shares of sales in key accounts first?"

"Exactly."

It's counterintuitive, for sure. "Then why wouldn't you start at the very bottom? Show them your hypothetical projected sales had you maintained the status quo. Show them doomsday."

"That's exactly what I'd do." He jerks back his head of thick dark hair. "I'm impressed."

"Really?"

He blinks at me appreciatively, and I notice that his eyes, which once were the color of tombstones, now seem more like...I don't know. Beautiful. Not a shitty gray on a shitty overcast day, but more like freshly polished silver.

*Or chrome? Oh shit.* I quickly think of his bike and its very flat back tire. I should say something. "Mr. Brooks, I have to—"

"Call me Nick."

*Nick.* It makes him seem so much more human and less Antichrist. Nick is the guy you hang with who has your back. Nick is the guy who tells you like it is out of respect.

"Nick." I nod.

He smiles, but this time his eyes are beaming. Like he's more than proud. Like he admires me just a little.

*No way.* The man is a bastard. But then why do I get the impression he's pretending to be this coldhearted jerk, just like I'm pretending to be Sydney Lucas?

"What?" he says.

"I-I don't know." I look away and squirm in my chair. I'm not used to anyone beaming at me. I generally don't even let them look. I'm like a goddamned turtle.

He grabs my chin and forces me to meet his gaze. "What's your story, Sydney?"

His touch sends a wave of…of *something* new through my body. It reminds me of riding a roller coaster—pulse, stomach, and head all in a twirling frenzy. It's a rush.

"What do you mean?" I ask, forcing my voice to stay even.

"I can tell you're used to being pampered and haven't worked a day in your life until you got here."

"I'm not a princess, if that's what you're implying."

"Then?" he asks.

"Why are you so interested all of a sudden?"

He shrugs. "I'm your boss. Why wouldn't I be?"

"Okay then. My story is that I'm shy, so people generally misinterpret it the wrong way—like I'm a child. Helpless. Incapable. Ignorant."

I see the startled expression in those silvery eyes

with thick dark lashes. Maybe because I've confessed something so personal. Even I'm shocked by it.

"Well, you'll just have to show them what you're really made of. Like you did with me," he adds.

I stare for the longest of moments, noting how his once cruel lips now look like sensual beacons, drawing me in. The planes of his cheekbones, which made him seem harsh, now feel alluring. The jaw, covered in a day's worth of dark stubble, no longer makes him look sinister, but virile. But above all, it's the look in his eyes that threatens to make me forget the very real fact that he's an a-hole who doesn't hold back. He'll squash you if it suits him.

"Don't look at me like that," he says.

"Like what?"

"Like you hate me."

"I don't...hate you." *Not anymore.* Though, I can't understand why.

"Good. Because I don't hate you either." He says it like he means so much more. But how can that be?

Suddenly, the door flies open, and Henry is standing there with fury in his green eyes.

# CHAPTER THIRTEEN

"Henry, nice to see you again." Brooks stands and goes over to shake my brother's hand; meanwhile, I'm behind my boss, shaking my head and mouthing, "You don't know me. You don't know me."

Henry's frown shifts to neutral, and I sigh with relief.

*Hold on. Why the hell did I just do that?* I should've just let the cat out of the bag right then and there, but now I don't want my charade to end. I want to stay and keep learning from Brooks. *I must be a closet masochist.*

"Let me introduce you to Sydney Lucas." Brooks gestures to me. "She's my new intern and was kind enough to stay late and pull together the information you wanted."

I can see the lost look in Henry's eyes—same green color as mine. He's a big guy, six five, dark blond hair like my dad, but Henry wears it messy, whereas my father is a crew-cut man.

"Your intern…Sydney?" Henry says skeptically.

Brooks looks away, and I'm behind him, nodding eagerly.

"Yes. She's quite smart. We may have to keep her after the internship is over." Brooks looks at me. "If she survives." He winks.

Henry draws a deep breath. "Uhhh…best of luck to you, then, *Sydney*."

Brooks gestures toward the doorway. "Let's go into the conference room down the hall and take this fresh intern out for a test drive. Shall we?"

I know Brooks doesn't mean it in a sexual way, but the muted anger in Henry's eyes is clear as day to me. He does not want anyone testing out his little sister.

"Yes." I step in. "I'll be gla-gla-glad to show you what I d-did." *Fuck. Stop stuttering, bonehead!* I swoop past the two, grab my laptop from my desk outside, and head down the hall.

I hear Henry and Brooks chatting as I set up and talk myself into a calmer state. This is not how I imagined proving myself to Henry, but it's now or never. *I can do this. I can do this. For my family.*

Henry enters the room, and I flip on the projector I've connected to my laptop.

"Ready, Mr. Walton?" I say with a raised chin.

"Ready when you are."

I did everything Brooks said, starting with the team's projected sales for the last two quarters, then working toward the results—the bad news followed by the good. Henry is quiet as hell with flat lips and stiff shoulders. No doubt he's in shock because he never imagined finding me here doing real work.

Okay. It's just a stupid report, but in the context of Georgie Walton, it's the equivalent of watching warrior squirrel fly a fighter jet.

The meeting ends, and we say goodbye to Henry, who says he'll be in touch next week.

"Good job, Sydney," Brooks says as I pack up my things and he heads out for the day.

"Thank you, Mr. Brooks."

"Nick." He flashes a quick smile and starts walking away, stopping suddenly and turning. "Oh, and, Sydney?"

"Yes?"

"I, uh…I'm sorry." His tone is sincere and remorseful, which makes me wonder if I've dozed off at my desk and I'm dreaming.

"For?" I ask.

"For being rough on you."

*Rough? Dude, I've met industrial sandpaper softer than you.* He was downright hostile.

He adds, "But for the record, you handled it better than I could've, which is an unexpected surprise—*you're* an unexpected surprise. A very good one, in fact."

*Wow.* It's a sweet, heartfelt compliment and something I never expected. It hits me right where it counts, like an ego-boosting arrow straight to my heart.

"Umm…thank you?" I want to ask why he was so mean to begin with, but I'd be pushing my luck. Frankly, I just want to take this win and walk.

"Oh. And by the way," he adds, "just so we're clear. I have not forgiven you for cancelling my return flight, cell phone, and company credit card."

My jaw goes slack. He knew? *No. Lucky guess. He's just fishing.*

"I have no idea what you mean."

He grins. "Uh-huh."

*Dammit.* He knows-knows. But how?

I watch him disappear down the hall into the elevator. Before I leave, too, I make a pit stop in the bathroom, where I am proud to say I will not be crying. "Not today!" I do my special version of the double-fingered disco-dance, complete with gyrating knees. "Who's awesome? Me! Me! That's who! That's who!"

Sadly, the janitor breaks up my one-woman party.

"Oh, uhh…don't mind me. I'm just Jazzercising." I scurry to the elevators, and when I finally get outside, it's a cool spring evening in downtown Houston, the sun having just set behind the wall of skyscrapers. I'm almost to the garage three blocks away when I hear a deep voice call my name.

I stop in place. *Oh no. Brooks.*

I turn slowly and watch him walk toward me; those broad shoulders and tall body move with strength and confidence. He definitely has a "don't fuck with me" vibe.

*No. Wait. He's just pissed.* I shrink on the inside as he walks up.

"You wouldn't happen to know anything about my bike and a flat tire, now would you?" he asks.

I pucker my lips like a naughty child. "Nope."

"You're a terrible liar." He points his finger in my face. "Last time, Sydney. No more revenge."

I nod submissively. "Yes, sir."

"Nick," he corrects. "Now you have the pleasure of giving me a ride home since I'm already late—I'll have to call roadside service in the morning."

I have to drive him home? I know he could just as easily call Uber, but he wants to punish me.

"Well?" he says.

He's waiting for me to lead the way to my car. *Oh no. My car.* I think fast. I'll just say it's my mom's.

When we get to my outrageously expensive BMW, Brooks—Nick—doesn't seem too surprised. In fact, he just cocks one dark brow and gets in.

"So, Sydney Lucas," he says once we're out of the garage, "what brought you to PVP?"

*Oh crap.* It's Q & A time, and I can't escape. "Errr…a friend at school told me about it."

"And why aren't you in school right now?"

"Um…I'm on a leave of absence this semester. I, uh…had a bad cold and missed the first few weeks of classes, but I'll start up again in the fall."

He nods, looking ahead and not at me, thank God. I actually enjoy driving, but only when alone. There's something soothing about feeling insulated inside my car, yet at the same time feeling like I'm part of this big busy world.

"And your major is?" he asks.

He'd know that if he'd bothered to look at my résumé. It still boggles my mind that he hired me without a second thought.

"Business. My father forced us all into it." Sounds pathetic now that I just said that out loud. "But I think I'll change next semester."

"To what?"

"Not sure yet," I say.

"Stick with business. You're a born salesperson."

"Ha!" I laugh. "Funny."

"I didn't intend that as a joke, Sydney. You have natural credibility, and you can be quite charming when you're not busy crying in the ladies' room."

*Yeesh.* "You heard about that?"

"The entire floor heard."

*Wonderful.* "Well, I don't cry because I'm sad or my feelings have been hurt—I mean, it does happen, but I generally cry when I'm frustrated and the words won't come out."

"You seem to be doing okay now."

"I'm only allergic to strangers, but fine with people I trust," I say. "It's always been that way."

He looks at me with a puzzled expression that borders on pleased or flattered or shocked—a suppressed smile, a twinkle in his eyes. "You…trust me."

It's not a question; he just doesn't quite believe it.

I give it some thought. It's true, I'm suddenly able to speak and function like a normal human being around him. But do I trust him? Christ, I don't know, and if I do, I can't for the life of me understand why.

I shrug.

"Don't do that," he says.

"What?"

"Shrugging is for the weak. It means you're unsure or insecure, and neither benefits you. Especially a woman who wants to build a career in the business world. Nobody likes a shrugger, least of all me."

*Ah. And there's Mr. Meanie Pants again.*

"Take this off-ramp and hang a left toward the Houston Tower Suites," he says.

*Swanky.* The Houston Tower Suites is a luxury condo community at the edge of downtown. It's pricey. I know because we have a fundraiser every year in the rooftop event-suite. In fact, it's coming up next weekend. Claire was going to cancel it given everything that's going on with my dad, but Henry insisted we keep it "business as usual," and that includes doing our charity work.

"Here we are." I pull up to the front security gate.

"I would thank you for the ride," he says with a

little smirk, "but we both know this wasn't exactly a friendly favor."

Meaning, I messed with his bike.

I smile awkwardly. "Thanks again for today."

"You're welcome…" He's about to say something else, but stops and shakes his head, like he's just chastised himself.

Finally, he looks at me, and our eyes lock. Suddenly, I feel my heart racing, and a rush floods my body. It's sexual. It's hungry. It makes my stomach knot but in a really good way.

"Goodnight, Sydney." He opens the door and gets out, shattering the intense moment.

I whoosh out a breath. "Nite." And I watch him walk away, noting the taper of his broad back into a fit waistline. I like watching him walk, I realize. There's a masculine sureness and confidence in his step, like he owns the world and will crush anyone who attempts to deny him.

I suddenly imagine what he might look like shirtless in a pair of shorts. *I bet he's got nice abs.* Yeah, he seems like the type to take pride in himself.

*Wait. What am I thinking?* I shake my head, berating myself, when my phone buzzes. It's Henry. *Oh, God.* I knew this was coming, but it doesn't make it any easier.

I hit the button on my steering wheel. "Yes?"

"Get your ass to my place, Georgie. We need to talk."

"What's with everyone telling me where to put

my ass? It's not public property, last time I checked."

In the background I hear Elle yell at him, too. "Don't talk to her like that, you big butthead!"

"Who else is giving your ass directions?" Henry snarls at me. "It'd better not be that boss of yours."

I sigh. "Where are you?" Henry has one place downtown. The other is near Austin U, which is pretty far. Sometimes, though, they stay over at Elle's house about an hour from here because her mother's in treatment for a brain tumor. Ironically, she's taking a super drug from PVP that's helped her make significant improvement. Elle has been working to increase availability of the drug but says she keeps getting pushback from manufacturing— some difficulty in sourcing the raw materials. It's a pity, because the prices are also ridiculously high, and Elle says she can't fix it until new formulas are put into place, which could take decades, according to PVP.

"We're downtown tonight," replies Henry. "Had some meeting in the city, as you're aware."

I'm aware. "See you soon." I am not looking forward to this conversation, but it can't be avoided. My only hope is that Henry will understand why I did all this.

"Are you out of your fucking bleach-blonde head!"

Henry bellows as he paces his living room, while I'm seated on the couch. I feel like I'm being scolded by my father.

I lean back and cross my arms. "Don't lecture me, Henry. This is your fault. You and Claire and Michelle."

"Our fault?" He points to himself.

Elle comes from the kitchen, sets a cup of chamomile in front of me on the glass table, and sits next to me with her mug. "Why don't you hear her out before jumping down her throat, Henry?"

"Why are you taking her side?" Henry grumbles.

"I'm not," Elle argues. "I just want to understand why Georgie would do something so uncharacteristically sneaky."

I look at Elle. It's hard to believe she's actually younger than me. She's got the soul of a sixty-year-old woman and the brain of Einstein, all packaged in the body of a twenty-year-old.

"Go ahead, Georgie," she says. "Tell us why you decided to take an internship under an assumed name at one of our companies."

I draw a breath and tell them the entire story, being sure to include every detail. When I get to the part about messing with Brooks, the two of them look horrified.

"I had no idea you were capable of being so nasty," Henry says. "Remind us never to get on your bad side."

"I'm more worried about this Brooks guy. He can't stay there," Elle says.

"But no one's complained about him," Henry points out. "I checked with HR. A clean record. In fact, his team seems to like him. All of them."

*They do?* I wonder how it's possible.

"What have you heard, Georgie?" Elle asks.

I shrug. "I haven't met many people on his team. They're all over the US, and Brooks travels to see them most of the time."

"You must've heard something?" Elle says.

"Abi said he's got a reputation for being a scary asshole, but that everyone still wants to work for him because he's some sales god."

Henry lets out a groan and scrubs his face with his hands. "Either way, Elle is right; I gotta fire the guy. He can't go around talking to people like that, least of all my little sister."

*Fire Brooks?* If you'd asked me this morning, I would've said, "Can his ass!" But now I know he is my dragon. Or my guru of hard knocks. Or my—crap, I don't know what he is. I just know I want to work for him. With Brooks, I've made more progress in one day than I have in my entire life with my shyness.

"If you don't want to promote him, that's one thing. But don't fire him," I say.

"Why not?" Elle asks with a bite. "He treated you like garbage."

"I'm fairly sure he's nicer to his garbage than he

was to me, but he forced me to stand up for myself. And now he's actually being kind of nice—he even apologized." I can hardly believe it, but there's a human being underneath all that wicked, cruel hotness. Still, I'm puzzled by it. Something just doesn't feel right about him. The abrasiveness then the kindness. He wasn't even mad about my little pranks. In fact, he seemed kinda happy.

Henry shakes his head. "I won't lie. I was pretty damned shocked when you presented those numbers."

"Well, I wanted to prove to you guys that I can help," I say.

Elle elbows Henry. "See. I told ya."

"So what are you proposing?" Henry asks. "I let you keep working for that asshole?"

"That you let me keep learning from him. Just for a little longer. Then you'll move me to Algae-Tech." That's our new biofuel company. "Under my real name, of course."

"Oh. I love it!" Elle claps. "She can be my wing girl!" Elle's been spending a lot of time with the team there, preparing to move the company to their next phase of going commercial.

"And what about school?" Henry asks.

"I've just got to take the finals from last semester, and then I have a year left. I'll work part-time until I'm done." Unless I change majors. But after Brooks's comment, I do wonder if maybe he's right. I might be a good salesperson.

"Henry," I say, "I'm not asking. I'm telling you I'm staying. And from now on, I'm helping you guys. I won't be shoved aside and patted on the head."

"I never patted you on the head. You ran away too fast," he says.

I nod. "True. But not anymore."

"I hate to say this," Henry rakes a hand through his blond hair, "and I know you don't like talking about what happened with Dad, but part of me wonders if it didn't change you for the better."

I don't know the answer to that. All I know is that it changed me. "Then we have a deal?"

Henry nods yes. "But if that fucker steps out of line with you again, he's toast and you're out of there, Georgie."

I absolutely know that Brooks will step out of line again. I expect him to. "Let's set the bar a little lower. And I will leave when I say it's time to leave."

Elle smiles proudly at me. "My wing girl!"

# CHAPTER FOURTEEN

*Two and a Half Months Earlier.*

"Georgie was right," Michelle whispers as we reach the beach in a matter of minutes, which is all we have. Any second now, they'll discover we're missing. The only thing going for us is the cover of night, and unfortunately, that's also going to make it difficult to find a boat.

"I think we should go that way." I point north. "If we move along the shore, the waves will cover our tracks."

"Great idea, honey," says my mom.

We turn and stop with a gasp. A wall of men is standing there with rifles pointed at us. I can't see their faces, just the silhouettes of their naked bodies and guns.

"Shit," I say.

"Where do you think you're going?" asks the man in the middle.

"Snipe hunting with you pervert geniuses," says Michelle.

"Aren't you the comedian," he replies. "Now let's not make this any harder than it has to be. I'd hate for one of you to get hurt."

"Right this way, ladies." One of the men turns on his flashlight and starts back the way we came. I keep thinking I should run for it, but what if they shoot? Or worse, shoot my mother or sisters?

We march through the trees, but instead of going back to our huts, they make us take another path.

"Where are we going?" my mother asks.

"You'll see," calls out the man from the back.

I'm scared as hell, my body tied up in knots and my stomach cramping. I am *almost* shocked that my father would have us hunted down like animals, but not really.

We reach a large structure that looks like an old warehouse with cement walls and a steep metal roof. The lead man opens the door and holds it for us. One by one, we go through, and I enter last with the armed men behind me. The first thing I notice is my mother with her mouth hanging open.

My eyes follow the direction of her gaze. *Holy crap*. It's my father. Naked. Standing on a little platform that has this strange-ass throne made of wicker. *Wow. That is something I really didn't need to see.*

"Girls, cover your eyes," says my mother. "Chester, this lunacy has gone far enough! You let us go this instant."

I agree with her about the letting-go part, but I cannot look away. Because my father isn't alone. He has a dozen women, all of them naked as the day they were born, kneeling at his feet like he's some beer-bellied, streaker god.

*Oh, but that's not all.* Mr. Naked Yoga has his posse of a hundred people assembled in the room, and sadly the fluorescent lights hanging from the ceiling's beams are extremely bright. I've never seen so many dicks, butts, and nipples, nor do I ever care to again. For a shy person like me, this is my worst nightmare.

"Remove their clothes!" my father calls out. "Their initiation starts tonight! They will each be wed!"

*Scratch that. There's my worst nightmare.* I step back, only to have my clothed ass cheeks smoosh up against a man's bare dong.

"Ew!" I jump in place, nearly falling.

"Chester!" my mother yells. "I know you've lost your mind, but our girls are not about to strip naked in front of your tribe of nudie morons and be married off!"

My father glares from across the room. "I am king here, and my word will be followed. You will all strip, pay homage to my greatness, and be wed to the man who maintains downward dog the longest," he says to my mom.

If it's batshit crazy to orchestrate a plane crash and kidnap your own family, it's fruitcake-fucked-up to marry off your own wife. As for the obligatory nudity, well, there are no words.

The men behind us start to move, and I think they're going to descend upon my mother and try to take her clothes. But that's not what happens.

*Ohellno.* I gasp as half the men in the room, naked as babies, some with very hairy asses, bend over to create an ocean of dangling hairy balls.

"They are all just so…" my sister Michelle blinks, "naked."

"Yeesh." Claire can't seem to look away either. "I'll never eat frank n' beans again."

"It's the nakedest train wreck I've ever seen," my mom mutters.

"Nasty." I hold back a gag. This massive butthole exhibition is the sort of thing one cannot unsee. But while I'm standing there, trying to process what's happening, I realize there is only one way in and out of this nearly empty warehouse. It's a double door with the steel handles on the outside.

I lean toward my mother, who is standing closest to me. "Quick. Pretend you're stripping, and take off your bra."

My mom gives me a look.

"I chucked mine," I say. "Too dirty." Seriously, I have small B cups anyway, and the guards have only been giving us the minimal amount of water. We used ours for drinking or underwear washing. "Hand it to me, and then run for the door." I turn and give my two sisters a wink and then glance at the door. I think they understand, but I'm not sure.

My mother unhooks the back of her bra, followed by the sleeve action, and then in one swift motion hands it to me.

"Go!" I yell and start pushing my sisters, who are following my mother. I stumble outside behind them. "Help me push the doors shut!"

All four of us lean hard, giving me just enough time to tie the bra around the handles, sealing everyone inside.

"Brilliant work, Georgie!"

"Go! Go!" I yell.

We run like the wind. In the dark. If that wind had no shoes on. But this time, we don't hold back. Now we know what we're up against. *The nut farm.* Pun intended.

Time passes in a blur, and I have no clue how long we've been running or how far. All I know is that all four of us are stumbling our way through the thickest, most grueling vegetation imaginable. Thorns, branches, and whatever ever else nature has to offer in the form of pain.

"Look!" Up ahead I see a light. Then more. *Headlights?* "A road!"

We make for them and spill out of the trees onto the edge of a highway.

"What the fuck?" Claire belts out.

The cars are zooming past us as we stand there like wet dogs lost in a storm.

"I don't believe it. I don't fucking believe it." I

look at the road sign ahead and then at my mother. "We're in Tampa."

Within seconds, like a miracle, a highway patrol passes and stops for us.

The nightmare is finally over.

# CHAPTER FIFTEEN

*Present Day.*

After Henry's, I spend the night tossing and turning, replaying my conversation with him and Elle while thinking about Brooks. In all honesty, I can't shake the feeling that I didn't do him justice. I portrayed him as a monster. Yet, in my heart, I sense he's not who he pretends to be. Nevertheless, when I told them about the things he said and did, even I couldn't make a case for the man. It's difficult to supersede facts with gut feelings, even if my gut tells me the man is smarter, nicer, and better than he portrays.

Or maybe that's what I want to believe? Because then I wouldn't feel like a crazy person for wanting to keep working for him.

I roll onto my back and stare at the faint light from my alarm clock shining on the ceiling. I'd planned to move to an off-campus apartment, but after my own personal episode of *Naked and Afraid*, I changed my mind about venturing out on my own. It's a comfort thing, and only my mother is in the house now. I don't want to leave her alone just yet, though Claire is just down the road. Michelle and Chewy live about an hour away.

I whoosh out a breath, thinking about how hard this has been for everyone—the kidnapping followed by this painfully public power struggle. I know Henry and Elle think we'll prevail, and maybe we will, but I don't believe they've considered what comes next.

Do we really want to run this enormous empire?

Sure, we wanted to safeguard these twenty companies from my father, but that's over now. He can't touch anything because he's locked up. So why are we holding on to a dream that was never ours?

Again, I don't know, but I question this path we're on.

Speaking of paths, my mind drifts back to Brooks for the hundredth time. "*You are a natural born salesperson.*" I wonder if that's true, because, if so, I think I'd like to sell a fresh start to my family.

It only takes a moment for my mind to produce an image of what my life might be like if we were truly free. I see Henry and Elle's children running through a big house and a Christmas tree piled high with gifts. I see Michelle with a big stomach, laughing and kissing Chewy as they expect their first. I see my smiling mother holding my new baby boy. And when I look to my side—

*Gack!* I catapult upright in my bed. *Ohellno. I*

*am not having babies with that man! Over my cold
dead body!*

"Did you have a good weekend?" asks Brooks as I
shuffle past him in the office on Monday morning,
avoiding eye contact.

"Sure. You?" I take a seat at my desk and get out
my laptop, hoping he doesn't notice the shame on
my face, because, sadly, after I finally fell asleep on
Friday, I spent the next two nights having very
sexual dreams about him—us riding naked on his
bike while we faced each other and screwed. I have
no idea who was driving. Then there was the dream
where he popped out of a cake, all covered in
frosting, and I licked it off. Even down there.
Oddly, in my dream, he tasted like grape cough
medicine, which I hate. Okay, maybe that dream
made sense. But the hardcore humping did not.
*Ugh. How awful.*

"What did I do?" he asks rhetorically. "I went
drinking, whoring, and sword fighting—the usual."

I look up, wondering if I heard correctly.

"The Medieval Festival," he explains. "Palo
Verde Pharmaceuticals is a sponsor. 'We're taking
medicine out of the dark ages and into the healing
light.'"

"Is that really our slogan?" It's so corny.

"Yes." He tosses a folder onto my desk. "And

here's the rest of the PR bullshit you should familiarize yourself with for Friday's fundraiser."

My heart drops through my chest into my stomach, and the two start boxing. "Fundraiser?"

"The Waltons give it every year, and some of our biggest clients will be attending. Do you have a formal dress?"

I have more dresses than I know what to do with, but no way can I go to an event we're throwing, and I certainly don't want to derail my progress. A party is exactly the sort of thing to send me into a tailspin back to my old ways.

"No," I lie. "Guess I can't go." *Please don't make me. Please don't make me...*

"Well, borrow one if you have to because I need you there. You'll be assigned to the rep from Phillipe Morrissey. He's a bigger asshole than me, if that's even possible, and thinks he's entitled to be surrounded by the most beautiful women in the room at these events."

Did Brooks just insinuate I'll be one of those women?

No. I'm sure that's not what he meant. Still, I can't help feeling a teensy bit flattered. Okay, a lot flattered. Suddenly, I'm seeing myself walk into the room filled with glamorous people. My chin is held high; I look amazing and confident. Then, like a scene from a movie, my eyes meet Brooks's. The desire in his eyes is instant and—

*Gah! What am I thinking?* I do not want my

boss. I'm confusing desire with the desire for his approval. Still, now I kind of want to go.

"You mean Philip Morris, the cigarette company?" I ask to change subjects in my head.

"No, Phillipe Morrissey. They're some depressing goth, French-herbal, health-kick-bullshit vape company. They buy our organic menthol compounds. The rep is Gerard Boucher, a self-proclaimed ladies' man—though I'm sure women everywhere would disagree."

"Wow. I'm so...excited to meet him?" I know I've just turned the color of a snow cone without the fancy rainbow syrups. Being pawned off on a man, clothed or not, gives me horrific flashbacks of tropical dangling hairy-berries.

Brooks tilts his head to one side. "You okay?"

I nod.

"Then why the hell did your face turn white? No. Wait. Now you're turning Kermit green."

"I wasn't aware he has an official shade, but I'm fine." I blink way too many times.

Brooks lets out a groan and places his beat-up leather backpack on my desk. I like that he uses something with so much character to tote his things, but I don't like him invading my space, apparently, because now my heart is beating faster than ever.

I take a calming breath but only manage to get a good solid whiff of Brooks's cologne. He smells delicious. *Delicious. What's gotten into me?*

"Sydney," he says, planting his strong arms on

my desk, "you know you're part of my team, right?"

I nod, gazing into those eyes that no longer seem like soul-sucking gray but mildly hypnotic. I feel myself leaning toward them.

"Good," he continues. "Because I would never put you in an unsafe position. I assigned Gerard to you because if I don't, he'll be bothering the rest of the women all night, and I know you'll keep him in line."

"Me?"

"Are you not the same woman who read me the riot act of anti-dick swinging in front of our president and then proceeded to leave me stranded in New York?"

I look down at my hands. "The, uh…stranding happened before I yelled at you."

"Either way, you can handle yourself."

I shrug.

"Oh no, no, little girl," he says, that deep voice filled with disapproval. "What did I say about shrugging?"

I glare at him. "Did you just call me a little girl?"

"And there you go, proving my point. You're tougher than you look." A sly smile curves his lips.

I sigh with exasperation. He did that on purpose to provoke me, and I somehow can't say no to this man. But now it's not because I fear him. I kind of *like* him. Platonically, of course. A one hundred percent, non-romantic sort of like.

"You play dirty, Mr. Brooks."

"Nick," he corrects yet again. "And it doesn't mean you can't trust me."

*Now he's pushing it.* His behavior hasn't been all knights in shining armor and castles. He knows it, and I know it. "If you say so."

He shakes his head, and this time I can tell he's not faking his disapproval. "If you doubt me, then get your stuff and leave. There's the door. Because if you ever feel unsafe, then the exit is exactly where you should be heading. Someday, I'll tell the exact same thing to my d—" He cuts himself off.

"To your…?" I wait.

"My…dry cleaner. She's a very nice woman. Good with impossible stains, but some of the customers are a little rude."

He was *not* going to say dry cleaner. He's lying. But why?

"Well, I'll see you Friday."

"Where are you going?" I jerk to my feet. I sort of hate the idea of not seeing him, but only because I'm here to learn and nothing else. I mean, what sort of stupid woman would want to smell his sadistic cologne while she sits next to him, going over boring numbers. He's way too abrasive. And I certainly don't want to watch him walk away so I might catch a glimpse of his muscled ass in those nice-fitting pants or imagine what he might look like if he were lying between my thighs, coming while I watched in a mirrored ceiling—

*Georgie! Whatthehell? So now you're a porn star, wanting your bastard boss and a creampie cameo?*

"Gack!" I shake my head.

"What's the matter with you?" His brows shrug together.

"Nothing. Never better, sir."

"Nick," he says with a little growl. "Sir makes me feel like I'm your father, and we both know I'm not him."

For a split second, I wonder if he's referring to the fact that he knows Chester Walton is my dad.

"I'm not that old," he clarifies.

*Phew.* He doesn't know, thank God. Because I'm not ready to give up this internship. There's still so much to learn. *Yes, yes. That's why.*

"You're what, twenty?" he adds.

"Twenty-one just last January." I celebrated in a hut somewhere in Tampa. There wasn't any champagne. Or cake. Not even strippers. *Because everyone was already naked.* I push away the unpleasant thoughts.

"How old are you?" I ask.

He glances down at the floor. "Old enough to know better. See you Friday." He goes into his office and shuts the door behind him.

I don't understand what just happened between us, but that was one hell of an awkward conversation that felt more like a weird dance.

*And I stupidly enjoyed every bit.* I rub my face and groan. *What am I doing?*

The week passes at an excruciatingly slow pace even though my boss is out and he's sent me plenty to do from the road, such as preparing the presentation for the next quarter's reports. All easy, but I notice the numbers, quarter over quarter, are insanely good. *Another twenty percent in growth?* Good for Brooks, but the best companies in the world don't grow that fast unless something major has happened, like taking on a big new customer or acquisition or something. But when I compare the amount of customers, they're pretty much the same. Seems most of the growth is coming from three pharmacy chains in the US.

*Huh.* Sitting at my desk, I rub my chin. I'll have to ask Brooks about that later.

*Brooks…* My body jolts with unexpected anticipation, and an image of those intimidating gray eyes and sensual lips slides inside my head. My pulse quickens, knowing I'm going to see him tonight. It's like some uncontrollable part of me is craving the rush I feel when we're in the same room. Yet, at the same time, I'm anxious in a bad way, too. He's been extremely curt when he calls, and his emails are suspiciously cold.

*Is he upset with me?*

*Get over yourself, Georgie. Were you expecting winky and kiss emojis?* Yet I can't help feeling like something's up, and I wonder if it has to do with his comment: "I'm old enough to know better." Does that mean he's been having thoughts he shouldn't? And why the hell does that make my stomach all fluttery? He's a man who, I'm sure, only wants outgoing, detached women that like it hard and rough. I've never even been with a man.

*I wonder if he can tell.*

*Oh my God. Stop it*, I scold myself. If I didn't know any better, I'd say I'm acting like I dig this a-hole. Am I forgetting what type of man he really is? I deserve better and kinder, and I definitely need a man who won't be rough with me.

I shake the thoughts from my head and start shutting down for the day. Brooks is giving a speech at our fundraiser tonight and asked me to check it over, write out his note cards, and bring them along.

I still can't believe I'm doing this. My brother and sisters will be there, but have reluctantly agreed to ignore me. "*It'll be like every other event I've ever gone to with you guys*," I wrote in a quick text to them. "*Just pretend I'm not there.*" I got back all sorts of written eye rolls, but they didn't argue.

I quickly finish the note cards for Nick and grab my things to dress in the ladies' room. I did my hair this morning in a simple bun, making my blonde hair look sleek and elegant versus its normal boring ponytail or braid down my back. I'll throw on a little extra mascara to make my green eyes pop and some shimmery red lipstick. It's my standard gala look. Only tonight, I'm not wearing a black "please don't notice me" sack-style dress. I'm wearing a formfitting red thing with delicate spaghetti straps. The hem nearly touches the floor and requires three-inch heels. The sequin beading around the low-cut bustline, however, is what makes the dress so sexy, and it's giving me second thoughts. Do I really want everyone noticing that part of my body?

I feel the panic creep in and the comfort of keeping to the shadows beckoning me. It's one thing to stand up to Brooks, but it's another to mingle at a big party with strangers looking at me.

*Maybe this is a mistake. Someone might recognize me.*

*Nobody is going to recognize you*, I argue with myself. Not a soul on this planet has ever noticed me at one of my family things because I usually end up standing behind a plant. I've literally bumped into my father's friends at their country club when I play tennis with my mother from time to time, and they walk right past me. Not even a smile. And trust me, my father's friends are—I mean, *were*—complete ass kissers. They'd all go out of their way to rub elbows with the Waltons.

I think I'm safe on the recognition front, but my heart still says otherwise. *Oh no.* And now it's protesting and...*I'm not going.* I begin to hyperventilate. I feel the eyes on me, judging. *No. No.*

I will have to tell Brooks I'm not feeling well. He won't care anyway.

I pick up my phone and text him. He's probably

at the party already since he lives right there in the building.

> **Me:** *I can't make it tonight. Sorry. Not feeling well.*

There. It's decided. I shut off my laptop and grab my dress and tuck my phone inside my purse just as it rings. I pull it out and see it's Brooks.

*Crap.* He's going to yell at me. I decline the call and go to tuck it away again, but then a beep lets me know he's texted.

> **Brooks:** *Why aren't you answering?*

I stare at the tiny screen. I can always lie and tell him I was driving and couldn't answer.

No. Stupid. He's seen my car. It's got Bluetooth, Wi-Fi, and hands-free everything, including shoe shopping. Not that I use it.

My phone rings again, and I freeze with the thing in my hand. I hate myself for it, but I want to hear that deep voice. I almost crave the shivers that run down my spine when I hear it.

"Hello?" I say.

"Where are you?" His tone is a notch below pissed off.

"Leaving the building," I say sheepishly.

"Are you dying?"

"No."

"Fever, vomiting, bleeding from your ears?" he asks sharply.

*I'm working up to it.* "I just don't feel well and—"

"Then you're coming."

I bite my upper lip. I don't like his tone. I don't like that he's demanding I come.

"No." This time I'm firm. And dammit, yay me!

He growls on the other end. "Sydney, why won't you come? The truth."

*The truth?* There's no point telling him because he'd never understand what it's like to have this thing inside you that you can't control. I've made progress, and I take pride in that, but it doesn't mean I'm cured. And trust me, I want to be. It's painful to be this shy. It literally makes my heart and stomach ache.

I sigh. "I'm not…I'm not…good with being in public."

"God help me," he grumbles with exasperation. "I'm coming to get you."

"No! No, I don't want to see…" *you.* I suck in a deep breath, suddenly realizing that it's not just the public and their staring eyes I'm afraid of. It's him, too. I suddenly fear walking into that room in my red dress, trying to look my most beautiful and bold, only to have him ignore me or not see me or not notice that it's all to impress…*him.*

I let out a groan of trepidation. How in the world did I get all crushy over this man?

"Too late, I'm already here," says that no-BS voice.

I look up to see Brooks standing there in a tux,

looking absolutely breathtaking—tall, elegant, those wide shoulders filling out his sleek black jacket to perfection, and his stubble adds just the right amount of roughness to his exquisite face. His silvery eyes seem paler tonight, and his thick black lashes look darker. *He's wickedly beautiful.* And I can't look away despite the swirling in my stomach.

"What are you doing here?" I ask.

"Had a tux emergency—missing button. My tailor is across the street." The frown is instant as he looks me over in my plain black skirt and blue blouse. "Where's your dress?"

I lift the garment bag draped over my arm.

"You do realize you actually have to put it on, right?" he says.

I nod, but on the inside I'm fighting like hell not to cry. Like I told him, it's not always about sadness for me. Sometimes the tears are the only way for my emotions to come out when I'm in a mental gridlock like this—I want to speak, but my body refuses.

Maybe he sees the torment in my eyes, or maybe he just wants to get me moving, but he lets out a long breath and rakes his strong hand through the side of his dark hair. "All right, I'm out of my league here, Syd. And I don't claim to understand what's happening inside that head of yours, but I can see it's something unpleasant." He lowers his voice and speaks with tenderness. "So just tell me what you need, and I promise to do my best to help. But I'd really like it if you came with me to the fundraiser."

I stare in disbelief. He didn't demand, bark, or belittle. Instead, he gave me a glimpse of his soft side. *This is the real him, isn't it?* I don't know why I think that, but tender suits him.

Suddenly, I feel myself falling, the attraction overwhelming. Because the fact is, *that* is what I needed. A man who can shed his armor for me, but at the same time show me how to wear my own. I just wish I knew why he goes around masquerading as a complete asshole.

One thing is for certain, I won't ever find out if I hide in my room.

I pat the side of my head, checking if my hair is still in place and party ready. "Thanks for the..." I don't know what to call it and not end up sounding corny. "The pep talk. I'll go put on my dress."

He smiles, and it's warm and sexy and inviting because those boyish dimples are on display. "See, I knew you just needed to hear the right sales pitch."

"That was a sales pitch?" Of course it was. And there I go again, acting like a naïve, wide-eyed little girl. *I'm such an idiot. He doesn't actually care about me.*

"Don't make it sound so dirty, Sydney. I gave you a little nudge of encouragement."

"I think I'll pass on the party. Goodnight."

His eyes follow me as I walk by him and head toward the elevators. "Sydney." I feel his strong hand on my wrist, pulling me back to face him.

"What just happened?"

I'm furious and getting more pissed by the minute. Not at him, but at myself. I think I want him to be good because then I won't feel like a fool for feeling an attraction to this uncaring beast.

"I have to give you credit, Mr. Brooks. You really are a great salesman. Because for one second, I actually believed you gave a shit about me."

He almost laughs, like it's the most ridiculous thing he's ever heard. "Is that really what you want, Sydney? I should hope you have larger aspirations in life than to have some asshole like me care about you, because I certainly think you can do better."

It takes a moment to realize what he's really trying to say: a man like him isn't good enough for me.

"Another sales pitch?" I ask.

"No. The truth." He leans down a little, putting his face closer to mine. "You're smart, Sydney. You're beautiful and young and you have your whole life ahead of you. Don't waste it on men like me."

His words are a plea to walk away, but his tone says the opposite: "*Waste your whole life on me.*" And, dammit, if there isn't a vulnerability in his eyes that makes me think he's way more damaged than he lets on.

*I can't even…*Not with this. The argument he's made only draws me to him again. It proves that deep down inside, while he might not be good, he certainly isn't bad. A bad man would try to take advantage of a woman like me. Men in power do it all the time.

"The problem is I'm really sick of people telling me what to think." I look him in the eyes, and the rush pumps through my body. "And I'd like to decide for myself how I spend my time or who's worthy of it."

"That *is* a problem." He looks down at me with a tick of torment in his eyes. "Because that sort of stubbornness makes it all the more difficult for me to leave you alone."

Before I can process what he's just said, he slides one arm around my waist and pulls my body into him. His hand cups the back of my head, and his lips are an inch from mine.

I can't move or breathe—no, not true. I'm panting, savoring the feel of my breasts pushing against his chest, three layers of fabric between our skin. The ache between my legs is instant, and I don't even care that we're standing in the middle of our office, where anyone could walk by and see us. I want to drink every salacious drop of the lust in his eyes. I want to soak it in like a brine that will preserve the moment forever in my memories.

Brooks's lips are so close, I can feel his soft breath on my face, but he doesn't move. *Kiss me*, I think over and over again. *Because we both know I'm not bold enough to do it.*

He abruptly lets go and steps back. "I'm sorry. That shouldn't have happened."

I want to say it's okay, that I want it, but he doesn't give me the chance.

"I'm your boss, and I don't take advantage of women, no matter how beautiful I think they are. Especially ones I'm supposed to look after."

My body goes cold with shock. "I don't need you to look after me," I say quietly, disappointed that he feels this way. He's attracted to me, yet thinks I'm too fragile, too weak.

He straightens his tie, and I imagine he's wanting to straighten out something in his pants, too, but won't dare do it in front of me. "In my profession, trust is everything, and we're not stepping over the line. You're not my plaything, Sydney."

"I know," I whisper. But is that what this is? I don't believe it for a moment. Not after his speech about me deserving better.

"I'll give you a ride to the fundraiser. I'll wait downstairs while you change—don't take too long."

As he walks away, I want to say that I know I'm not some goddamned ball-busting, fiery woman who approaches life with a knife in one hand and grenade in the other, ready to crack skulls and take names. I know that's what society wants me to be, but not all women are like that. Some of us are gentle and kind, and yes, a little shy. But that doesn't mean we're not smart or powerful in our own way. Power is about being yourself, accepting who you are, and finding strength in that. Some of us do it quietly, and others do it with blazing guns.

The point is, just because I don't wear my emotions on my sleeve and spout off every thought inside my head doesn't mean he'd be taking advantage of me. Yet the fact that he cares so much about it makes me want him.

# CHAPTER SIXTEEN

When I get outside to the front of the building, I notice the awaiting Town Car with the back door open. Brooks is inside, sitting on the leather seat closest to me, talking on his cell. He doesn't even watch me approach, but I'm not surprised. Not now. Because now I know he's trying very hard not to notice me.

I slide into the car, my ass scooting past his face since he's decided to take the seat closest to the curb, and my mother taught me to never enter a vehicle on the traffic side of a busy street. "Always get in on the side closest to the curb. That is safest and where a lady enters."

"What if someone is sitting there?" I asked.

"Then they're ill-mannered. But you are my daughter. You stick to etiquette and, above all, your safety, Georgie. There are bad people out there who wish to harm you."

"Why?" I asked.

"Because the have-nots want to blame the world and resent us. Sometimes they want to hurt us."

I don't remember agreeing, because I spent my time with plenty of people who had less—my teachers, other students, the staff in our home and even the people in our social circles. When you're a Walton, few people are richer than you. Still, I suppose some of my mother's common sense stuck, and that's why I'm trying to scoot past my boss while I'm in a skintight red gown and three-inch heels.

As I baby step my way past him, his hand grazes my backside. I can't tell if it was an accident or he just couldn't resist.

I go with the latter, because after what just happened back there, I'm on fire. My crush has turned into scalding hot lust, and I don't know if it's because people inherently want the things they can't have or because he feels it's his duty to follow a strict moral code when it comes to touching me. It's a potent, sexy, tempting combination, and my body is making it blatantly clear it now wants him. My breasts feel fuller against the snug fit of the dress. My hips feel tighter. My panties feel constricting. Every inch of me is pulsing to break free and invite his touch.

I take my seat, the driver closes the door, and we're off. Brooks is still on his phone, giving the occasional "uh-huh" while I try to ignore the energy buzzing through the air.

He shifts slightly, giving me a wedge of his back. The tension in his shoulders and neck mirrors my own.

*What would happen if we both relieved it?* I don't know, but I really want to find out.

When the car slows, I can't believe we're already here. This time, Brooks gets out first so I don't have to climb over him, though I'm not sure I'd mind.

He turns and holds out his hand while the other is still stuck to his phone. I wonder if he's even talking to anyone at all? Feels like a convenient way to ignore me and shove away any libidinous feelings.

I take his warm hand and exit the car, but he looks away and immediately lets go once I'm no longer at risk of tripping.

*Fine. I can play too.* I keep walking, ensuring Brooks has nothing to look at except my ass in this dress. When I get to the elevator, I turn, but he's nowhere to be found.

*Son of a biscuit!* My confidence takes a hit. Here I am thinking I'm tempting him with every weapon in my lady arsenal, and he's run off to be with his mistress: work.

"Hi, I am Gerard Boucher." I look up at a redheaded man in a tux.

"I'm Sydney Lucas." I politely nod.

"Oh. Sydney." He takes my hand and kisses the top, lingering just a bit too long on the skin. "I am from Phillipe Morrissey. I was looking forward to meeting you, and now I know forward is the wrong direction."

"Sorry?" I say.

"A man does not move forward for such a beautiful creature. He falls."

I jerk my hand away. Brooks was not joking about this guy. He's a sexual octopus, ready to get his tentacles on me.

The elevator chimes open, and I step inside, pushing the rooftop button.

"So, I understand you are new to PVP?" he asks on the ride up.

"Yes. I'm an intern."

"Ah. Such a sweet time in one's life. So young."

*Eww and eww.* "Not so young. Not so sweet."

"Ah, but much to be learned." He wiggles his red brows.

*Ick! Not from a scum trunk like you.* Thankfully the doors open, and when I step out, Henry is standing there greeting guests. I head straight for him.

"Mr. Walton, so nice to see you again," I say.

There's a flicker of outrage in his eyes. "Delighted to see you again—*Sydney*, was it?"

*And big brother's hating on me. Big time.* I am unsure why, so I move quickly to Elle, who hugs me and whispers in my ear, "You're out of your fucking mind coming to this party in that dress."

I pull away. "Huh?"

"Every man here is going to be hitting on you. Henry won't stand for it."

I pfft. *Yeah right.* "Your husband is an idiot."

"My husband loves you more than life itself,

little Georgie," Elle hisses. "Don't you *ever* forget it."

I've never seen Elle mad, and it puts me in my place. "I'm sorry. I didn't mean it that way. I know he loves me."

She gives me a nod of forgiveness. "Then don't make a scene tonight. I'm all for your self-exploration, but none of us, including you, can afford a scandal. You've all been through enough."

"I understand." I smile politely and wander off through the crowd of tuxes, jewels, hairdos, hair don'ts (are bouffants really back?), and expensive ball gowns to find champagne. I don't normally drink, but I need to take the Brooks-edge off. I'm wound so tight, I might snap and break out in a spontaneous twerk to release the pressure.

I go to the bar and feel a warm hand on my back. I turn my head, deflated it's not Brooks.

"Hello, Gerard. What can I do for you?" I say inhospitably.

He leans down to whisper in my ear, "You are the most stunning woman at this party. Every man is looking at you, and I too am raptured by your beauty."

*Oh boy.* Coming from any other man, I might take that as a compliment. But his sticky suction cups are pressing on my bare back.

*Off, damned octopod! Off!* I step away.

"Do I offend you?" he asks.

*Offend isn't the proper word.* Revulsion is more

like it. "No."

"Then why is your beautiful face the same shade of red as your dress?"

The mere fact that he has to ask is a sign of his utter senselessness. "I need to powder my nose."

I shuffle off down the short hallway that leads to the restrooms and to the terrace doors. There's a magnificent view of Houston's skyline out there, and I know because I've spent hours hiding there over the years. But tonight, I'd really like to stay in the light. I want to show the world that even the quietest women can be brave and strong. Brooks needs to see I'm able to hold my own.

I head to the ladies' room to freshen up, and when I come out, a hand snatches my arm and jerks me outside through the door.

"Gerard?" I push away from him.

"Oh, please. Do not tell me you don't feel it, the animal attraction. The desire burning through you."

"The burning you sense is my desire to vomit. Likely on your shoes. Let go." I jerk my arm away, and he grabs me by the waist.

"Oh, come now, my little dove. I know you ache for flight."

Did he get his romance training on the bottom of a cereal box? Because…damn. It's cheap. And so underwhelming.

"Why don't you take a flying-dove fuck off?" I say.

My refusal only seems to animate him. In the groin. Because I feel an unwelcome poke through his pants against my dress.

"Gerard, let Sydney go."

I turn my head, and there's Brooks.

Gerard releases me and goes inside without so much as a word. He clearly fears my boss, and he should. Nick Brooks is a large, well-built, and intimidating man.

*And he's in so much fucking trouble!*

"You okay?" Brooks asks.

My nostrils flare, my fists ball, and my muscles pump with adrenaline. Gerard has riled me up, but not in a good way. "No. And how fucking dare you. You said to trust you. You said I'd be safe! Well, I wasn't. And he's…*icky!*"

"Icky?"

"Yes! Why would you put me in that position?"

He shakes his head. "I'm sorry, Syd. But you held your ground, just like I said you would."

*Oh my God.* "Is that what you think I wanted? To hold my ground against some rapy Pepe Le Pew?"

"He's offensive, but totally harmless. And it's good you learn how to *not* let assholes take advantage of you with their smooth talk—it's a lesson you needed."

*Wait.* "This is about you, isn't it? You're making some fucked-up point about keeping men like you away, because of what you said earlier. Of course, nobody gives a shit about what I want. Isn't that right? I'm just some little girl who needs big strong men making decisions for her."

"No."

"Then why all this? Why the speeches and weird lessons?"

The harsh emotion dissipates from his handsome face, and his hard planes soften along with his lips. "Because someone needs to be the grown-up and ensure nothing ever happens."

Between us, he means. "And that someone should be me?"

"Yes."

*There he goes again. Thinking for me.* "Forget that!" I throw my arms around his neck and plant my lips on his. *How's this for a lesson, Brooks?* He's my dragon, and I want him to admit that he can't make choices for me. No one can. Not anymore.

His hands go to my arms, and his body goes rigid, but he doesn't push me away. I wait, drinking in the warmth of his lips, the two of us breathing each other in. I can feel him struggling to give in. Then he slides his arms to my waist and kisses me back. His silky lips move against mine, and his tongue glides into my mouth. My body lights up. It's just a kiss, but it feels more intimate than anything I've ever imagined.

"Stop." He pulls away, and just like that, the kiss is over. "Is it out of your system now?" he says coldly, like he didn't even enjoy it.

"Not even close. And I refuse to be baby-fied."

*Is that even a word?*

He grabs my chin and shakes his head. "Then you can't work for me anymore, Sydney."

"You're firing me?"

"You don't understand," he says in a low voice. "You have no idea what you're getting yourself into."

"I know that you're not as bad as you want people to believe. And that—"

"Sydney, you're only going to end up hurt."

"Why?" I ask.

"Because I'm an asshole."

"I already know that. So again, why?"

He makes a little growl of frustration. "Because believe it or not, I like you too damned much. And if you ask for more of an explanation, you're not getting one. It's for your own good."

"I'm not a goddamned child," I snap.

"In my world, yes, you are."

*Wow.* I can't believe it. *I've had just about enough of him, the world, everyone saying how helpless I am.*

The rage is instant, and before I know what I'm doing, my palm is flying through the air toward his face.

He catches my hand in midair, and I try to jerk it away so I can land a good one. "Let go!"

It happens in a split second, but his cufflink catches the delicate satin strap of my dress and the thing just snaps.

I look down, and my breast is out there. *Oh shit!* It's just…there, my pink nipple staring Brooks right in the eye.

Now, this is the part where most women would place their hand over their boob, gasp in horror, and run off to the bathroom, never to be seen in public again. Because, ohmygod! I am flashing my entire left boob to my boss. But we're talking about me, the girl who locks up like a bad pair of brakes when anything remotely overwhelming happens.

I'm standing there, unable to react as my entire nervous system shuts down. Brooks looks down at my breast, and his mouth gapes open just as a couple walk out onto the terrace. I'm absolutely certain he's not thinking straight and that the blood in his brain has gone to some other extremity because his instant reaction is to shield my naked body.

With his hand.

"Jesus! I'm so sorry, I—" Brooks jerks his hand away, and then, horrified that he's let my boob out again, he plants his other hand over it. "Oh! God. I'm—" Fumbling with his hands, Brooks lifts up the flap of my dress and covers me by pressing it to my chest. Only now it looks like he's just fondling me through the fabric.

"Brooks, get the fuck away from her!" Henry's voice rages through the air.

"Ohmygod!" Elle rushes toward me to take over

boobgate, and I turn my head just in time to see Nick Brooks meeting the full force of two hundred and sixty pounds of defensive end muscle known as Henry Walton's fist.

Brooks flies back and lands with a grunt.

"You're fired, Brooks," Henry roars. "Don't ever show your face in any of my companies, let alone the state of Texas, again."

I want to tell Henry that he's wrong and it only looked way worse than it was, but I'm stuttering my words and Henry's too angry to listen.

I watch Brooks dust himself off and leave without a fight.

*Shit. Why did I just let that happen?* It feels uglier than anything Brooks ever did to me. Who's the asshole now?

# CHAPTER SEVENTEEN

It's been two days since Henry fired Brooks, and despite my efforts, no one will listen to me. Not even Elle, who's pissed that our night, which should've been about pediatric cancer research, turned into a tabloid scandal. *"Mystery girl is attacked at Walton fundraiser."* Fortunately, the lighting wasn't so great on that terrace, so my face is all pixelated. Unfortunately, the light hit my boob at just the right angle when Brooks reached for it, and someone tweeted the security footage. #BoobGate-Gala is born.

Regardless, I can't argue. I let it all get out of hand, and now Brooks's career is in the toilet.

*I can fix this. I can.* Henry will hear me if it's the last thing I do when I go to his house tonight for a family gathering. I just need Brooks to know I'm not letting him drown. I once let it happen to a man who deserved it, but Brooks doesn't. And no, the irony isn't lost on me that I'm now trying to save the job of a man I was once hoping to have sacked.

I pull up to the Houston Tower Suites and give

my keys to the valet.

"Are you a resident, ma'am?" he asks.

"Just visiting." I'm about to take my valet ticket when I spot Brooks a half block down on his Harley, shooting from the garage.

"Never mind." I grab my keys, hop in my car, crank the engine, and tear after him.

A half hour later, heading east, I'm sure I've lost Brooks. His bike has no issue weaving through Sunday afternoon traffic, whereas I'm quite possibly the slowest, most polite person on the road. My driving says: *Um, excuse me? Would you mind moving, please? No? Okay. Then I'll just wait.*

*Show some backbone, girl!* I use my brights, followed by me waving while mouthing, "I'm so sorry. Emergency!"

*It worked!* I grip the steering wheel, but when the obstacle moves, Brooks is no longer in the fast lane.

I look around the stretch of highway and spot him taking the next off-ramp. "No!"

I make a split decision and jerk right, across four lanes, nearly slamming into a semi, who flips me off with a very loud horn and a finger out the window.

"Sorry!" I yell.

As I get to the off-ramp, I see Brooks ahead hanging a left at the green light.

*Shit. I'm going to miss it.* I hit the gas, but by the time I get to the intersection, the light is changing from yellow to red.

My tires screech as I take the turn anyway. *Crap. Crap. Craaap!* I make it, but only because the driver entering the intersection saw me coming and slowed.

"Sorry!" I wave. "I'm a horrible person!"

With my focus back on Brooks, I spot him up ahead, turning right.

*No!* I won't see where he goes after that.

Praying I'll get lucky and find him anyway, I make a right into a residential neighborhood filled with older but well-maintained ranch homes. The gardens have flowers and neatly trimmed hedges. The lawns are mowed. Tricycles are left unattended in driveways, and a few trees have tire swings. Immediately I know this is a family neighborhood, which makes me believe that Brooks is here to visit friends or something.

Just as I think I'll never find him in this labyrinth of courts, lanes, and streets all named after flowers like lilacs, buttercups, and tulips, I see Brooks's bike parked along the curb.

I slow my car, cautiously approaching. If he were to see me, I'd feel pathetically stalker-ish.

With no cars behind me, I come to a complete stop. Four houses down, Brooks is standing on the lawn, holding a little girl with dark curls. She's got her arms wrapped around his neck and laughing.

*Is she his niece? Or perhaps goddaughter?* But I notice he's holding her so tight that there's a desperation to it.

He finally sets the little girl down, and that's when I see her. A woman my age who looks like the girl. *Wait. She looks really familiar.* I just can't place her. I then look at the little girl, and though it's from a distance, I think she looks like…Brooks, too. Same nose. Same shaped eyes.

*Ohmygod. Is that his daughter?*

The woman smiles, overjoyed to see Brooks, and embraces him. I see the love in his eyes for her.

*Fuck me. That's his wife.* Or, at the very least, it's the mother of that little girl, and no one is acting estranged or unfriendly. It's a picture-perfect scene of daddy coming home after a long road trip.

The reason he wanted me to stay away suddenly makes sense. *He's living a double life. He's not single. He really is an asshole.*

By Wednesday, my life is unraveling at all four corners. Sunday's family dinner at Henry's turned out to be a huge shouting match. Okay, they shouted with their mouths, and I shouted with my eyes. Nobody wanted to listen about Brooks, but mostly because I defended my ex-boss—a man who was caught bare-handed, cupping my bare boob at a charity function, only adding to the list of atrocities he's committed, including making fun of my clothes, my mother, and making me cry in the bathroom.

Don't get me wrong. If one of my sisters told me her boss had said and done those things, I can't claim I'd be sympathetic. Regardless, I hadn't been trying to defend him because I am beyond heartbroken to find out he has a secret family. Why the hell wouldn't he just say the truth? However, my only intent Sunday had been to explain to my family that the fundraiser was a big misunderstanding. The real reason to hate the guy is far bigger, but no one would let me get a word in, and then I just got upset, so I left.

Monday, work was a cluster because everyone was talking about Brooks being fired and boobgate with some mystery girl, who most assumed was me. Abi could do nothing to get me out of the bathroom, but I couldn't care less about that or Brooks being fired now. I was wrapped up in the image of him holding that sweet little girl and his wife—girlfriend—whatever. My anger, hurt, and disappointment came from one thing and one thing only: I believed in him, even if for a brief moment. But I should have believed him, *not* in him, because he warned me about the type of man he is. He just didn't give the details.

Tuesday was worse than Monday in that my anger turned into a mental rehash of every tiny detail since I met the man, including that kiss. Now I can't get the feel of Brooks off my lips. Their softness, their warmth, the lust penetrating my skin. How could he kiss me like that if he's in love with someone else? Then the university called and said my approval had come through. I could finally take my tests and put this whole chapter behind me. The only downside is that I have to come today and test for all five classes. Ten hours straight, starting at seven a.m. My counselor told me to contest the short notice, but I'm ready to move the fuck on with all of it. The kidnapping, the legal battle, my internship, and Brooks.

Which leaves me here on a Wednesday evening, sitting in an empty classroom, rereading the biggest piece of crap ever written about revolutionaries in Latin America for my world history class: *In conclusion, they fought. They fought hard. They wanted equality. They also wanted the power for themselves. They wanted to be the masters of their universe, and what the hell am I writing?*

*Ugh!* I start erasing and write down some PC crap about man's inherent right to freedom. It's bullshit because "man" will never be free. We have to share this fuckball of a planet with the Brookses of the world.

I drop my pencil, grab my backpack, and hand the festering pile of philosophic turds to my professor, Dr. Mills.

She takes it from me, reads the title, and frowns. "Fuck World History? Especially the History Part?"

I jerk my head. "You try being in a plane crash, kidnapped by your dad, and falling in love with your married a-hole boss, and then tell me what you think of the planet."

It only vaguely registers that I have just spoken a very full sentence to a stranger without issue. Go figure. Hating my boss—ex-boss—was the cure all along.

My professor slowly bobs her head. "I will give your essay my full consideration."

"Thanks." I walk from the classroom, ready to give tequila my "full consideration" too. I push open the classroom door and launch into a steady stream of students pouring from the auditorium directly across. I stumble and slam into someone.

"Oh! Are you all right?" says a soft voice.

I look up and see a familiar face. *Dear bajeezuz!* It's Brooks's wife.

I knew I recognized her. I must've seen her around campus. Maybe we even had a class together once.

"Ohmygod." She grips me by the shoulders. "You're turning green. Do you need an inhaler? Are you having a heart attack?" She looks over her shoulder at some random dude. "Call 911!"

I shake my head and double over. "No! No 911. I'm fine," I pant.

"You don't look fine."

"Looks. Can. Be deceiving," I sputter, my head feeling like it's trapped in a vacuum, lacking the proper oxygen.

She helps me upright. "Okay. Wow. I've never actually seen that shade of green on a person before."

"Totally fine," I croak. "I'm part frog."

She frowns. "Can I get you some water or—why don't you lie down for a moment." She points to a bench against the wall near the exit.

I anchor myself and stand tall like a weak oak. "I'm okay, really."

"Wait. Don't I know you from somewhere?" she asks.

*Yes. Your front yard. Sunday. You had your arms around the man who's literally driven me so insane that I'm forgetting all my prior insanities.*

"Nope," I say.

"Wait. Yes…I'm sure I've seen you before."

My fear tells me that she might recognize me as Georgie Walton, so I say the only thing I can think of. "Oh, wait. Yeah. I've seen you around my cousin's place. They just moved into a house down the street from you and your husband—the guy with the Harley, right?"

"Really? What a small world! But that's not my husband. He's my brother-in-law—I live with him."

My mouth cracks open. "I could swear I jogged by and saw you two together," I lie.

"Oh God no." She grimaces. "Sam is like a brother to me, and I'm engaged to my high school sweetheart. We're getting married as soon as I graduate next month."

*Sam? Who the hell is Sam?*

She adds, "Logan, my fiancé, is actually on the

east coast right now finishing his last semester of college. He'll be home right after finals."

Now I'm seriously confused. So Sam is...Brooks? Nick Brooks?

"Well, wow! Congrats. And excuse me for being nosy, but who's that adorable little girl?"

Her eyes fill with a forced neutrality. "My niece, Joy. I help Sam take care of her during the week ever since my sister died two years ago."

I want to cover my mouth, but I'm not supposed to know this woman or Brooks. *Or...Sam? Crap. He's been lying about everything, not to mention hiding the fact he has a daughter and is a widower.* My mind jumps to the easiest conclusion: the pain is too much and he'd rather not have people gossiping behind his back or saying anything to remind him of his deceased wife. I can't hold it against him, frankly. Making a career in the corporate world is tough enough. Having customers or coworkers pitying you or seeing you as "that poor man" would not help. My only question is, how did he get such a high-level job under a fake name? I mean, it's apples and oranges compared to me. I'm an intern, a temporary employee who's yet to be paid. Execs have to go through background checks, drug tests, and credit reports. I won't lie. It's suspicious.

I squeeze her arm and offer my sincerest condolences. "I am so sorry for your loss—umm...what's your name?"

"Erin."

"Erin," I repeat. "Well, it's nice to finally meet you. And again, I'm sorry about your sister."

"Thanks. I really appreciate that. Maybe you'll come by sometime when you're in the neighborhood? You can meet Sam. He's really sweet. The best, actually. And Joy, his daughter, is incredible. Do you have kids?"

*Is she scoping me out for a fix-up?*

"Nope. No kids." *In fact, I've just recently graduated from childhood myself.* This is the first normal, adult conversation I've ever had with a stranger.

"Well, Sam is only home late at night because of work, but he's usually around on the weekends." She shrugs. "If you want to stop by."

"Sure. Next time I visit my cousin."

"I hope you will." She takes my hand and squeezes. "Nice to meet you…?"

It's a split-second decision, but using my fake name doesn't feel right for two reasons: One, she's super nice and it feels wrong to lie again. Two, if Brooks is living a double life, then surely I'm not at risk of exposure on his account.

"Georgie," I say. "See you around."

"Hope so!" She bounces down the hall to the exit.

Once she's gone, it sinks in. Something strange is going on, and I have to go see Brooks. Or Sam? Or whatever the hell his name is, because without knowing the full story, how can I possibly fight to have him reinstated? The fucked-up piece of this is that part of me thinks maybe that's a bad idea. It certainly would avoid a bigger mess down the road in terms of liabilities for PVP.

I let out a breath and scrub my hands over my face. I never imagined that my horrible, hot boss would split me right down the middle, challenging my every thought, and making me question my own heart. I hate him, but I want him. I want him, but I never want to see him again. I never want to see him again, but I miss him. He's the worst, the best, and the hottest piece of work I've ever met. Yet, when it comes down to it, none of these glaring contradictions seem to override my gut, which is urging me closer.

# CHAPTER EIGHTEEN

"Hey! Sam! Open up. It's me." I pound on the door of his Houston Tower condo in the early afternoon on Thursday, hoping he'll be home.

In my head, it's all planned out: I'll ask questions to test his honesty. I'll figure out which side of me has misjudged him—the side that wants to trust or the side that wants to dig a grave and bury him in it.

At this point, I'm equally torn because I can't deny what I feel. He's changed my life, and regardless of the how, I'm grateful. Yet I'm loyal to my family and to myself. As a woman, I cannot accept or condone his offensive behavior. Yet I'm here. Standing at his door, willing to hear him out. Why would this man, a widower and father of a beautiful little girl, conceal his life?

"Brooks! Open the hell up or, so help me God, I will punch you in the face!"

There's no reply.

"Fine!" I yell. "But you grabbed my tit! And in my book, that means I'm entitled to a few answers, so if you won't open this door and face me, then you're not only a greedy fondler, but a second-rate douche! That's right! A knockoff vaginal cleanser from Dollar Fanny! Not even fit to stand beside the respectable douches found in CVS!"

"Wow. Are you done yet?" Brooks, who's standing behind me, crosses his meaty arms.

I drop my furiously door-knocking hand. "Where did you come from?"

He points over his shoulder. "From the non-crazy-person aisle just over there."

"Funny."

"What are you doing here, Sydney?"

I snarl with my eyes. "What do you think, *Sam*?"

"So you know." He exhales with a whoosh. "I figured this was coming."

I point toward his door. "You gonna let me in now, or would you prefer I rant some more in the hallway?"

He walks toward the door, inserts the key, and pushes. "Won't you come in?"

"Thought you'd never ask." I shove past him and proceed to his living room, a light gray and dark brown themed space with modernist, army green furniture. Looks like a chic lounge for the Special Forces.

"Someone loves his military hues," I comment.

Brooks shuts the door behind me. His wide shoulders stretch out his plain blue tee, making him look fiercely powerful. His black shorts have just enough tightness to accentuate his muscular thighs. He looks extra ripped today and insanely tense, like a man about to blow a gasket.

"Did you just work out? Because you look like you could use some more."

He frowns. "Why are you here, Sydney?"

"I think we covered that already, *Sam*."

He gestures toward his dark green couch. "Take a seat."

I nod and do just that. "So?"

He sits across from me in the armchair and leans back, manspreading his legs and taking up space with his large body.

I force myself to ignore what looking at him does to me.

"Well, what do you want to know?" he asks.

"Start with the easy stuff."

"None of it's easy."

I nod. "Okay, then start anywhere you'd like."

"I notice your shyness isn't an issue any longer. Why don't we start there?"

*Huh?* "Not sure what you mean."

He leans forward, planting his strong arms on his thighs. "It was all an act, wasn't it?"

"What? No." I pause for a moment, trying to find my bearings in this conversation. I don't succeed. "I'm not the one who's pretending to be someone else." Oh, wait. That's not exactly true. Either way, "Why don't you tell me what's going on? The truth."

"Why don't you tell me how you managed to botch up six months of undercover work when I was one week away from having all the evidence I needed to put those fucking monsters away."

*Errr...Paging diaper. Paging diaper. Please pick up the white courtesy phone. 'Cause I'm going to pee myself.*

"I'm so-sorry," I stutter. "Did you just say...undercover?"

He narrows those silvery gray eyes at me. "Cut the crap, Sydney. I don't have time for this and neither do you. Because you're going to fix this."

My mouth kind of flaps, but no sound comes out.

He goes on, "I have everything I need to bring PVP's president up on racketeering, extortion, illegal price fixing, and a dozen other antitrust laws. What I don't have is proof of involvement of the Walton Holdings executives. And you, Sydney, are going to help me get it."

My mind does this horrible whipping motion where I feel like I'm in the grasp of a giant who's thumping my body between two boulders. *Thump. Ow. Thump. Ow.*

*Henry. He's going after Henry. And Elle!* "But what did they do?"

"They killed my wife."

"What?" I jerk forward on the sofa.

"Let me paint the picture for you, Sydney.

Those greedy pieces of shit created a market short-age of their cancer drugs in order to drive up the price of a medicine my wife needed and couldn't afford, and the insurance company wouldn't pay for. Meanwhile, they are selling that same medicine on the black market to the highest bidders."

This is why PVP's profits have been growing hand over fist. They pretended there was less medicine available to max out their profit in the market, and then sold the rest to the wealthy. At least, that's what Brooks is saying.

He continues, "All they had to do was play fair and release the supply. They still would've made a profit and saved thousands of lives, my wife being one of them."

I'm horrified. Just…horrified. "I'm so, so sorry, Mr. Brooks—I mean, Sam. I truly am. But I don't think the Waltons had anything to do with it."

"Chester Walton was notorious for being closely involved with all aspects of operations. No one so much as sneezed at one of his companies without his approval."

That's actually true. It's why Elle and Henry had to jump through so many legal hoops and we were all left scrambling—still are—to manage this empire. My father structured everything in such a way that executives could only make tactical decisions. Big contracts, big payments, any strategic decisions went through him. I think it's why he went nuts. All that stress.

Sam continues, "And now there's strong evidence to suggest that Henry Walton is following in his father's same greedy footsteps because nothing's changed. They're still selling their drugs to what essentially amounts to pharmacies for the rich."

I know Henry would never do such a thing. Elle's mother is currently being treated for cancer with one of those PVP medicines, though I'm not sure it's the same one. Either way, neither of them would put profits over people's lives, and Elle has personally been trying to make our drugs available to anyone who needs them.

This is probably an opportune moment for me to tell Nick—Sam—that he's barking up the wrong tree. But then he's going to ask how I know, and revealing that I'm Georgie Walton will put me in the enemy's camp. He'll hate me, which breaks my heart. I don't want that, but I can see it's personal for Sam. The rage in his eyes means he won't listen to reason.

I sigh, feeling more torn than ever. He deserves his justice if what he says is true about Craigson—PVP's president—even if I know the scandal won't be good for my family. But I can't help him go after Elle and Henry.

*And maybe I can't go lying to him anymore either. This has all gotten out of control.*

I open my mouth to speak, but he cuts me off.

"Now, since you've managed to figure out who I am, and managed to get me fired—"

"You got yourself fired," I point out.

"I was only trying to help. What was I supposed to do? Let you expose yourself on the terrace?"

I blink. "You had a jacket. You could've put that on me."

"Fine. I reacted quickly and wasn't thinking. Not to mention you'd just kissed me and…" He throws his hands in the air, followed by a slow inhale. "I was trying," he says with restraint, "to do the right thing. Just like I am now. Which is why you're going to help us get into the Waltons' secure email server."

"Me? I don't know anything about hacking, and you won't find—"

"You hacked into my bank account, which is not only a felony, but another reason to do as I'm asking. Quietly."

I narrow my eyes. Oh, I see where he's going with this. Of course, it wasn't me who made his money disappear. It was Robbie, my friend from my computer sciences class, and I'm not about to rat him out.

I cross my arms. "Then send me to jail, Mr. Policeman."

"I'm FBI, not the police." He points to his wallet, which is sitting on the glass coffee table. "Go ahead; look inside."

I stretch out my shaky hand and look inside. The clear little window has an FBI ID with a picture of him on it.

I set the wallet back on the coffee table and slide back on the couch. "I can't believe this."

"You can. Just like you can believe I'll have you thrown in prison if you don't do what I'm asking, Sydney."

Wow. I just didn't think it was possible for Brooks to be a bigger a-hole. But, in his defense, he did warn me. Several times.

"Sorry," I say flippantly. "I'm immune to your assholiness now, so you can't intimidate me."

He groans. "Sydney, why are you making this so hard?"

I shrug. And then I shrug again just to irritate him.

"Stop that," he says.

I shrug once more.

"You're a real pain in the ass, you know that?"

This time, I add a spiteful smile to my shrug.

"All right," he says. "But know that because of your interference, some very bad people who killed my wife, the mother of my child, will likely get a slap on the wrist and nothing more. This is on you."

I can't shrug flippantly this time. It's too sad and the hurt in his eyes is too real.

"I'm sorry about your wife. I really am." It almost brings me to tears thinking about it. If those drugs could have saved her life, I can't blame him one little bit for how he feels.

"As am I." He nods stoically at the floor. "Well, I suggest you stay away from PVP tomorrow. It's going to be messy."

It's not lost on me that despite everything he's just said, he's still trying to protect me. My only question is why?

"So you're going to arrest Craigson. Then what?" I ask.

"Then we go after the other executives, and Henry and Elle Walton."

My mouth drops. "Didn't you just say that you don't have any evidence?"

"I said we don't have strong evidence. But we'll still do our best to get a conviction."

*Arrest Henry and Elle? Ohmygod.* It doesn't matter if they're not convicted of any wrongdoing, the arrest alone will destroy us. Not to mention it will ruin Henry's dream of the NFL. They tend to stay away from bad PR when possible. *Oh no. And Elle is pregnant. She can't go to jail.*

"Okay. I'll help," I say.

He gives me a suspicious look. "Why the change of heart?"

"Well, if they're guilty, as you say, then they should pay." But really I'm hoping I'll find evidence to prove Henry or Elle were lied to by PVP execs and that they are completely innocent. My stepping in is the only shot I have at getting Henry and Elle off the hook.

"Glad to hear you're on board," Sam says.

He's glad because he's unaware that nervous Nelly here is about to have a panic attack.

*Brooks is a fucking FBI agent. And he's after my family. And*—"Where's your bathroom?"

"Errr...down the hall. First door on the left." He points over his shoulder. "You all right?"

I make a run for it and get to the bathroom right before the big stomach cramp kicks in. I'm light-headed and my lungs feel like lead weights.

*Oh boy. FBI. FBI. How the hell is this happening?* I hang my head over the white porcelain sink, trying to breathe away the panic attack.

"Sydney? Are you sick?" Sam says, standing outside the door.

Panting, I run the cold water and start splashing it on my face. "I'm okay! Be out in a minute."

*Ohgod, ohgod, ohgod. He's after Henry and Elle. And it's up to me to stop him? What the hell are you thinking, universe!*

Several minutes pass and so does the noxious wave in my stomach. When I stagger out, Sam is leaning against the wall right outside the bathroom door. His bulky arms are crossed over his broad chest. He looks even tenser than before, like a protective pit bull standing guard.

"You all right?" he asks with an unexpected hint of tenderness in his deep voice.

I shake my head no.

"Don't worry," he says softly. "This will all be over soon, and then you can go on with your life."

*Go on with my life.* It sounds like he's really say-ing, *"You can forget you ever met me."* So was any affection towards me an act, a means to an end, to punish some very bad people in the name of his wife?

*Dammit.* I so want to hate this man, but once again, I find myself unable to. I genuinely sympathize with him.

"So what's next, Mr. Brooks?" I ask with a sigh.

"McDaniel," he says. "My name is Sam McDaniel."

I stare into those hypnotic eyes. "The name suits you." The hardness and determination finally make sense. Because Nick Brooks was an asshole. Sam McDaniel is a man with an ax to grind who clearly loved his wife. It's hardened him, and screw me, but I think his loyalty toward her only makes him more attractive.

*Are you out of your mind, Georgie? He wants to put your family in jail. He's not your friend. He's the enemy.* More importantly, now I'm sure he could never want me. I'm a Walton.

# CHAPTER NINETEEN

On Friday morning, as I'm poking the elevator button in the lobby, it quickly becomes apparent that I have dug myself into a deep, deep hole. *What am I doing?*

Brooks—I mean, Sam—wants me to log in to the system and hack into my corporate headquarters' server, find the secure server that's got some weird name, and then download a bunch of email folders. I'm fairly sure that what I'm doing is illegal, even for the FBI. Not that I know squat about squat when it comes to the law, but I do believe a warrant is required anytime someone's privacy is invaded.

*Or maybe not?* I am part owner of the company, and he's got me doing the hacking. It can't be illegal for me to dig around or take emails that belong to Walton Holdings.

Still, this feels so damned wrong, but it's either this or watch Henry and Elle get arrested. I'd warn them, but I'm guessing the FBI has anticipated I might and that they'd simply pass go and start arresting everyone.

I get to my desk and am immediately greeted by Rebecca, who tells me I'll be finishing my six-month internship with her. We set up a time to go over the projects I'll be working on. Once she's gone, I get to work.

Step one: call Robbie, who's raised his price to one hundred and fifty per hack.

Step two: give him remote access to my computer.

Step three: pretend I'm working while he logs into the server through some portal thingy and attempts to get through their firewall thingamajig through my laptop.

"I'm in," Robbie says over the phone.

"Great. Now what?" I ask.

"Read off the server ID to me."

I give Robbie the info, and through the phone, I hear him tapping away on the keyboard. Suddenly, a long script pops up on my screen, but nothing happens.

"Are you sure that's the right server name?" he asks.

"Yeah." I repeat it for him just to be sure.

"Then it's not here."

"What do you mean, not here?" I ask.

"Exactly what I said. And you're not getting your money back."

"Keep the money," I hiss. "Just find the server."

"It's not here. Maybe it's been shut down or replaced or who the hell knows? Look, I gotta go.

I'm playing *God of War* and Kratos lost his ax."

"Huh?" The call ends, and my computer screen shuts down. *I can't believe this guy!* If they had a Yelp for hackers, like Yackers, he'd be getting a frowny face from me.

I drop my head and groan. *Crap.* What am I going to do? If I tell Brooks—dammit!—I mean Sam, he'll just jump to his fallback plan: arrest.

*Okay.* I give it some thought. I know how badly Sam wants this, so I am going to tell him. Maybe they got the server name wrong. Maybe it's on some entirely different network.

I grab my phone and text him: *No go on the server-o. No chickens in the coop.*

Sam immediately responds: *I know.*

**Me:** *What do you mean you know???!*

**Sam:** *It was a test. Wanted to make sure we can trust you.*

I fume. *What an a-hole!* Does he have any idea of what I just went through? *Actually*…I pause, realizing I sort of feel fine. No urge to freeze up, cry hysterically, or hurl cookies.

**Me:** *Why? What's the plan?*

**Sam:** *Come to my apartment after work, Georgie.*

**Me:** *Ok, but—*

*Ohshit! Ohshit! He called me Georgie. He knows!*

My phone rings, and it's him.

"Ye-yes?" I say.

"You didn't actually believe the FBI would pick some random intern to help us, did you?"

*No. Maybe. Okay, yes!* "How long have you known?"

"Does it matter?"

Of course it does. I want to know if he's been playing me all along—the niceties, the encouragement, the kiss. Because his cover went way beyond just pretending to be Nick Brooks. He's always been after my family, and if he knew who I was from day one, then this was all just some big old mindfuck. The only thing I don't get is why he'd be so cruel to me at first.

"Yes. It matters," I say.

"Seven o'clock sharp. My place. Don't be late. And, Georgie, whatever you do, don't go running to your brother. He's already in enough trouble." Sam hangs up.

I glare at my phone. *What the hell?* I very literally want to throttle this man with my bare hands.

It's seven thirty by the time I get to Sam's door. Yes, I arrive late on purpose. I resent the fact he's been toying with me from day one.

"You're late," he says, opening the door. He's wearing a bruise on one chiseled cheek, faded jeans, and a plain black T-shirt that accents the swells of his pecs and large biceps. I hate that he's so good looking, even with a facial scuff. It's a total waste of a hot man body!

I close the front of my pink hoodie, feeling my usual vulnerability creeping in. "Yeah, well, I had to stop by the pharmacy for some Pepto and St. John's Wart."

He closes the door and raises a brow.

"My stomach and I aren't friends with stress, which you've brought to my life in festering, copious heaps," I explain.

"I'm sorry, Georgie," he says in a low voice. "It was never my intention to pull you into this."

"Oh no?" I poke his chest. "Seems like you knew from day one what you were doing." I narrow my eyes. "The flirting and whole fucked-up mentor-act. You're the worst. And what was the point of being so harsh with me? Because I know it wasn't to help me like you said."

"Yes, it was an act, but I did what I had to do. Can we not get into this right now?"

*So he did do all that on purpose! What a jerk!*

"No!" I shove at his chest. "You were heartless and cruel. You wardrobe shamed me and insulted my mother. I spent two full days bawling my eyes out in the ladies' room because of you, and now I find out it was some act. Why, Sam? Why put me through all that and then be nice to me and make me like you, only to fuck me again with this FBI bullcrap and threaten my family—who I know for a fact has nothing to do with any of this shit! Henry and Elle are good. Unlike you. You just hurt and lie and make me want you, and then you use it against me like some sexual monster, a monster of seduction. You should be disbarred. Or whatever they do to mean, hot FBI agents."

Sam looks uncomfortable—eyes shifting, upper-lip biting, and muted groaning. "Are you done yet?" he mumbles from the side of his mouth. "Because my team and I would like to go over the plan." He jerks his head to the right toward his dining room area.

I slowly turn my body to find three stern-looking men and one woman, all wearing plain T-shirts and jeans, looking oddly underdressed given their stiff, authoritative demeanors.

*Great.* They heard all that, including my confession of lusting after him. I run for the bathroom.

"It's a nervous thing. Just give her a minute," I hear Sam say right as I slam the door shut. I bow my body over the sink, once again feeling like my heart is about to explode and take my stomach with it.

"Georgie?" Sam steps inside and closes the door behind him.

"Go away." The last thing I need is to have him see me like this—sweating, panting, and my green eyes looking like Christmas ornaments with all that red in them. "I'll be out in a minute." I run the cold water and splash some on my face. Thankfully, my hair is up in a top knot today.

"I know this is a lot to take in," he places a warm hand between my shoulder blades and makes soothing little circles, "but you need to trust me now. I'm not the bad guy. I just need to get to the bottom of all this because it's the right thing to do."

I shut off the water and turn, my face dripping. "You're serious. You want me to trust you. Why would I do that?"

"Because you know you can."

"Oh really?" I throw my hands into the air. "Then why not just tell me what was going on from the beginning? Why the games and humiliation and manipulation?"

He shoves his hands in his pockets. "I don't work alone, Georgie. I have a boss just like everyone, and we follow protocols when it comes to figuring out who we bring under the tent."

"Fine. But that doesn't explain why you treated me like dirt and then acted like you cared."

"Of course I care. But I volunteered for this role because I have a personal stake in this. I committed to do anything asked of me. The asshole you saw was part of the job. Someone like Nick Brooks would never be suspected of being anything except a greedy, arrogant, egotistical prick. He's the first to break the rules. He's the last person who'd get upset over a few under-the-table deals—some of which he facilitated."

I chew on it for a moment. "You did all that for

show. So Craigson would trust you."

"Yes, and it worked. I showed him a guy who was just as soulless as he was, and he let me right in."

"And what about me?" I ask.

"You came out of left field. No one knew for sure, but we suspected you came to keep an eye on me, which would mean there was a very serious leak. We decided the best approach was to test you. We had to know."

*That's why he gave me the job so quickly.* I want to gasp and cover my mouth, but instead, I just stand there stewing.

He continues, "We—my team—all agreed that if it was a fluke, you'd bolt after a few days of abuse. But if you were there to spy on me, then you'd stick it out no matter how nasty I got."

The dots start connecting in my head. He wanted to run me out. "But I stayed."

"Yes. You sure the hell did. But when I took that trip to New York, I was really in Virginia meeting up with my team to decide what to do with you—take you into custody quietly so you wouldn't undermine our work, or feed you misinformation. But then," he shakes his head, "you pulled all that crap with the airline ticket and my bank account. That's when I suspected you had no clue who I was. No one working undercover would jeopardize themselves with sloppy sophomoric pranks."

I drop my jaw. "Excuse me, but they were genius and carefully planned."

"You gave your name to the credit card and cell phone companies. Your hacker friend used a computer from the university that had his log-in ID. But the hidden speaker in my office sealed the deal—amateur hour. The porn soundtrack was a nice touch though."

I thought all the ladies would complain to HR about Brooks watching porn in his office, thus mounting a case for his termination.

He adds, "FYI, my office was swept regularly for bugs. And no one trying to legitimately spy on me would be dumb enough to stick it under my drawer with watermelon-scented duct tape."

"I love that tape. It smells really nice. And I'm not dumb."

"No. You're not. You're very bright, Georgie," he says affectionately, his gaze falling to my lips. "And I'm not going to lie, I felt a certain pride when you stood up to me. I knew it was a big moment for you because you did not deserve to be treated like that. And for that, I am very, very sorry—for hurting you and…for everything else."

I could almost accept his apology if it weren't for that last part, which I assume is in reference to him making me believe there was something between us. For that, there is no excuse.

"Well, let me tell you something, *Sam*. I think your heart is in the right place, but I would never hurt people—good people—in order to get what I want. You misled me. You made me believe in you and—fuck me for saying this—but I started having feelings for you, which is why I went to bat to get your job back. And that's what makes you a horrible person. You're willing to leave dead bodies in the road to get what you want when there's another way."

"Georgie—"

"No." I shake my finger in his face. "You could have told me the internship was filled. You could have said I wasn't right for it, like the ten other companies who rejected me. But you made a choice to manipulate and deceive me. And yes, I may have lied about my name, but I never pretended to be someone else. But you! *You!* Put me in the middle of another horrific situation—a person who has had her life turned upside down, whose own father crashed a plane just to hide his grand kidnapping scheme. You may have lost your wife, and I know that hurts, but it doesn't give you the right to hurt me and to take away the only good I have in my life: my family. There is another way, Sam, but you're going after the jugular—my jugular."

Sam draws a deep breath. "I'm not going to argue, Georgie. You don't deserve any of this, but, frankly, I don't believe your brother or his new wife had anything to do with what PVP is up to. However, there isn't one person at the bureau willing or able to save your family from the avalanche of accusations about to come once we arrest Craigson and the other executives behind this bullshit. Henry, at the very least, will be taken down with them, along with your father, and I think you know I'm right. It's the reason you told Henry nothing and agreed to hack the server for us—you believed we wouldn't find anything."

It dawns on me; he wanted to see what I'd do. If Henry were involved and I knew it or had any doubts, I would have jumped to warn him.

"Georgie," he adds after a long pause, "not everything I said was a lie."

I fold my arms over my chest, waiting for him to elaborate.

Torment floods his eyes. "I really do think you deserve something better. You're a good woman. And you have a chance at a long and happy life. If you stay away from damaged men."

"Damaged. Like you."

"In the worst kind of way."

His words drain the last of my energy. I'm literally exhausted—with this situation, with him, with my own emotions—and I can't think straight. *I need Teddy, a good stress cry, and sleep.*

"So now what?" I ask with a sigh.

"Now you help us finish this. And you clear your brother's and sister-in-law's names."

"How?"

"You're going to help me break into your brother's safe and get a thumb drive."

# CHAPTER TWENTY

After I leave Sam's apartment, I'm driving home and get a call from Abi. She's been texting me about going to some housewarming party tonight. I'm definitely not in the mood. My head hurts, I'm worried sick about how everything will shake out, and most of all, I do not want to break into my brother's safe.

"I'm sorry, Abi; I can't go. I have to get up early for a family thing," I lie. Really, I'm supposed to see Sam to go over the plan, which is basically sneaking into Henry and Elle's on Monday when they're both back in Austin, where Henry is finishing up the semester.

"Come on, Georgie," Abi whines. "I really don't want to go alone—I won't know anyone there except the cute guy from my accounting class who invited me."

"He's an accountant, and it's a housewarming party. I'm sure you can handle a night of Scrabble and *Big Bang* reruns without me."

"Ha. Funny. It's actually his cousin's party, and

it's supposed to be a big deal."

"I really can't. I'm tired and—"

"Georgie, I never ask you for anything. Especially after the thing with your dad. I mean, I was just so glad you weren't dead. I literally cried for a month straight and could hardly leave my room after you disappeared. But the day my mom told me you were alive was the best day of my life. And since you've been back, it feels like you don't want to be friends anymore. You call once a week, and I've seen you for lunch a few times, but that's it. You don't text. You don't want to hang out. You're in some other place mentally."

I sigh. I know she's right. But how do explain that I'm breaking. I've taken all I can.

"I love you, Abi. And I'm sorry I've been so distant. I'm just worried, yanno? The stuff with my dad. The legal battle. My parents' divorce. Studying for makeup finals. My brother and sisters going out of their minds trying to keep the wheels on the bus." *And my horrible, hot boss who's really an FBI agent.* "But soon this crap will all be over, my family will be safe, and everything will go back to normal."

"Not too normal, I hope. I like the new you and how you're finally coming out of your shell. I just wish...I wish I could be a part of it, instead of feeling like some stranger watching from afar."

I get what she's saying. She and I have suffered from this affliction as long as we've known each other. Now we've both changed and have this opportunity to do the things we've always talked about—go on dates, socialize with strangers, get out into the world, be bold.

"Okay," I say. "I'll go to the party, but only because I love you, and I know you're not going to make me stay too long. I hate parties."

"Yay!" She claps through the phone. "But does the new you really hate parties? Or is that the old you?"

"Both. Definitely both. The last one I went to, my boob made a cameo in front of my boss, whose first reaction was to cover it with his hand."

She chuckles.

"It wasn't funny."

"Sorry." Abi snorts. "It's just, the man had ten other options to restore your modesty, but his first thought was to grab your tit? Sounds to me like he did the first thing that came to mind, because it was already on his mind."

"You're reading way too much into it." Sam has no interest in me outside of his mission to make PVP pay. Any feelings or affection he showed, including that panty-melting kiss, was all an act. Plus, he's still mourning his poor wife. I'm sure of it.

I start thinking of Erin, Sam's sister-in-law, and how she was trying to set me up with him. He's not the sort of man to need help getting a date. No, if he wanted to get back on the horse, he'd have women lined up, which leads me to believe that he's not ready. Although, when he lets his guard down, there's a look in his eyes that tells me he wants to.

*Maybe he can't.* Not until the past is settled. And if I were him, I wouldn't rest until I'd done just that. I know what it's like to want bad people to pay for hurting the ones I love. Sometimes I think if that pilot had been closer, I might've pushed his head under. Mercy for murderers simply isn't in my genes.

"I don't know, Georgie," Abi says. "I saw the way Brooks looked at you around the office. Those were not eyes of disgust."

I can't tell her the real reason he had been watching me: because he'd been *watching me* watching me. In the FBI sense.

"So, what time should I pick you up?" she asks.

"How about eight?"

"Great! I can't wait. Oh, and wear something chic and sexy. The guy who's throwing the party is some hot Australian swimmer, a Mitch something. He was on the cover of *Vanity Fair* last month."

"Mitch Hofer?" I ask.

"That's the one."

No wonder she wants to go to the party. Mitch is the latest new sports eye candy. He swam in the Olympics and then did some underwear ads in Europe. He's known worldwide for his excessive bulge. In fact, that's his nickname, "the Bulge."

"Can't wait to meet the swim-trunk legend in the flesh," I say. Maybe it will take my mind off

Sam and this enormous mess I'm in.

"The party's going to be epic. You won't regret it."

"Aren't those famous last words?" I say.

"Since when did you become superstitious?"

"Since everything stopped going my way. Over the last twenty-one years."

"Okay. You weren't joking," I say to Abi as we pull up behind the long line of cars in an Uber Prius. The other vehicles are flashy and expensive sports cars that go right up there with my BMW. There's security everywhere, paparazzi lining the street, and hordes of gorgeous people pouring in. "This *is* epic." Not the word I'd use, but I don't want to be a killjoy by telling her this is terrifying.

"It's going to be so fun." Abi is practically glowing with excitement, and I think part of it has to do with her outfit. She looks amazing in her short black dress and spiked heels. Her brown hair is flattened to a glossy shine. Everything about her is screaming "Tonight's my night!"

Then there's me—my blonde hair in a top knot, red lips, fake eyelashes, black heels, and a short green '50s-style dress with black swirls that flares out at the waist. It says, *"I'm here to have you look at me, but I'm not sure I'm going to like it."* Oh and, *"I like dresses that hide nervous spills."*

I groan. "I'll need tequila. Stat. Pronto. Lickety-split."

"I was hoping you'd say that."

"But we're only staying an hour. That's it, Abi. Otherwise, I'm going to freeze up or cry in a closet or something."

"Why can't you just accept you've turned a corner and have fun for once in your life, huh? I mean, you're twenty-one, you're alive and free. You've been through hell and back and came out on the other side." She grabs my arm and gives me a stern look. "You came back from the dead, girl. *The dead.*"

"You know what, you're right." I'm the only college student on the planet who's never had a good time. My world growing up consisted of being forced to attend fundraisers, polo matches, debutant balls, and making public appearances with my family. Of course, I hid in the kitchen or behind the first tree I could find. It was a nightmare. "I'm going to have fun tonight. I deserve it."

We thank the driver and step out onto the sidewalk, where a carnivorous pack of wild photographers screams to get our attention while snapping off photos in the hopes that we'll be someone worthy. Feeling like old times, my heart begins to race, and I shield my face.

Abi takes my free hand. "You got this, Georgie."

Do I? Do I really?

Yes, I got this. I am not backsliding into my old

ways. *Not today!*

I drop my hand from my face, turn toward the mass of flashes, and wave. "Drink it in, people!"

Having absolutely no clue who I am, they stop shooting.

"Wow. That did not go how I imagined," I say.

"They're idiots. Come on." Abi tugs on my hand, and we head to the front door. It's invite only, so the security guard, a big-ass dude in a black suit, checks Abi's name.

"She's my plus one." Abi points to me.

"Sorry, ma'am," he says. "But I only have *you* on the list. No plus one. You can come in, but your friend cannot."

"What? No!" she protests.

It's a sign. I'm sure of it. I'm not ready for parties yet. "It's okay, Abi. Really. Don't make a scene."

"Do you know who she is? Do you?" Abi says to the guy. "This is Georgie Walton. The heiress to the Walton fortune."

"She could be Elvis's long-lost Martian love child for all I care. If she's not on the list, she's not getting in."

I see the line of gawkers growing behind us. This is more humiliation than I bargained for tonight. "Thank you. Good night."

"Uh-uh, sister. You wait right there." Abi points in my face. "I'm going to go find Mitch's cousin. He'll fix this in a minute." She squeezes my arm. "Don't you dare go anywhere." She darts inside and disappears among an ocean of schmoozing bodies.

I step aside and try not to notice that people are staring and smirking at me as they pass.

*Oh, God. I am not doing this.* I turn and march off toward the street, but head right, away from the group of paparazzi. Sadly, there's another group in that direction, too. *Dammit. This is so embarrassing.* Everyone's going to know I didn't get in. Why else would I be leaving at 8:30 p.m.?

"Georgie!" I hear a deep familiar voice call out.

I turn and see Sam following behind me. He's wearing a tailored black suit and black tie. He looks like his usual big, badass, sexy-boss self.

"What are you doing here?"

He smiles, but it's the guilty kind.

"No. Please do not tell me I'm being followed."

"It's part of the job, but I also happen to know the host."

Do they think I'm going to run away or go blab to my brother? "Well, you can shove your job up your—"

"Eh. Watch that tongue, young lady. I'm not your boss anymore."

"So?"

"So that means you're not allowed to swear at me."

"Says who?" I ask.

"Me." His mouth curves into a sly, cocky little smile.

"Go away. I'm not in the mood for your fucked-up antics."

"Are you in the mood for a party?" he asks.

"Notice me marching to the nearest cross street to catch an Uber?" I turn and start walking. The photographers don't even seem to notice I'm alive because I'm not hiding my face like someone famous.

Sam catches up and starts walking beside me. "I happen to have an invitation and would love you to be my plus one."

"No, thanks. I'm good."

He grabs my wrist. "Come on, Georgie. Let me do this one thing for you."

I stop and face him, jerking my hand away. "I don't need charity from you, and I hate parties." I spent my entire life avoiding them because my dad just used them as a vehicle to parade us around like his little trophies of excellent breeding.

"Then why did you come here?" The headlights of a passing limo shine on his handsome, unshaven face, illuminating those chiseled cheekbones and strong jaw I love so much but now choose to ignore.

"Abi, my best friend, didn't want to come alone."

"So now you're abandoning her, huh?" His tone is riddled with judginess.

"Don't." I narrow my eyes.

"What?"

"You're trying to make me feel bad."

"I think you're capable of doing that on your

own."

I'm about to tell him to take a hike when my phone goes off, a text from Abi: *OMG! Where are u? Plz don't tell me u left.*

"It's your friend, isn't it? She's upset because you abandoned her." He tsks at me. "Not very loyal, are we, Georgie?"

That sets me off. I hate his condescending tone, and it's the last straw. The quiet anger that's been brewing inside me explodes. He messed with my heart. He messed with my life. He's messing with my family. Yet he has the gall to show up here and pull the "you're a bad person" card?

"What would you know, Sam McDaniel, about friendship? Or loyalty or anything? You're just some lonely, angry, middle-aged man with a bone to pick with the world, who goes around fucking up people's lives. For what? Does it make you feel better?"

His eyes turn cold, and I expect him to tell me to screw myself or scold me for talking down to him.

I wait, and then I wait some more.

"You're right," he finally says. "You're absolutely right. And no, it does not make me feel better. Nothing has since Kate died, and I doubt anything ever will. Except you."

I blink at him. I'm not sure I heard right. "Sorry?"

"The day you ranted at me was the first time in

years that I actually smiled."

"Why would that make you happy?"

He scratches his scruffy chin. "Maybe because you surprised me, or maybe it was because I caught a glimpse of the woman hiding underneath that shell. Maybe I liked seeing her."

I feel the swirls gathering in my stomach, and suddenly I can't remember why I was yelling at him just now. Perhaps I was mad because he'd faked his feelings for me, and somewhere deep down inside, I wanted them to be real.

But now, I'm not mad anymore. Or am I? "Another sales pitch?"

"No." He sounds offended that I'd even think it.

"How can I trust anything you say, Sam?"

"Ah." He nods. "Because I lied to you before. I manipulated you."

"Exactly."

"Well, I know someone else who lied. She even gave a presentation to her big brother and pretended not to know him."

*Dammit.* He's got me there. However, the difference is I meant it when I kissed him. I wanted him. Maybe I still do. But I can't say all that. I'm simply unable to express my emotions the normal way. My way is to start shaking like an incontinent Chihuahua.

*No. You're done with being terminally shy.* Ironically, I have Sam to thank for it.

I shrug. "Fine. I lied. But I'm not sure it's a reason to trust you."

"Valid point. In fact, if I were you, I'd be thinking right now that this guy is trying to get on my good side so I'll be more compliant."

"Nail on the head."

"Like I said before, you're smart, Georgie. But I also remember saying that you're young and beautiful and you have your entire life ahead of you, that you shouldn't waste any of that on an asshole like me. But…"

"But what?"

He shakes his head as if regretting what he's about to say, "But that doesn't mean I don't really wish things were different."

I look into those eyes, and they're filled with something potent that pulls me in. Hard lust. Hopeless desire. Need. I've never been looked at by anyone like that, like I'm so damned special they'd burn the world down to the ground just to have me. I think it's what I've been waiting my entire life for.

Before my brain catches up, my body is leaning towards him and his supple lips. He steps in close, and I feel the heat of his body pressed to mine. Suddenly, everything is moving slowly and the world melts away while memories of our first kiss flood my mind. And despite my fear of him and what he's capable of doing to my heart if I open it, I ache for him.

He stares down at me, and my eyes are locked

on his wickedly sensual lips. I feel it happening, me falling back into that hole I know I won't be able to dig myself out of. I want him even if he's damaged.

"If you really wish things were different," I say, my voice quiet, "then let them be."

He abruptly steps back. "Georgie, I wasn't lying when I said that it's never going to happen with us. Some lines can't be crossed, and you're—"

"Not some plaything," I finish his sentence.

"You're work. It's all you can ever be to me."

*Ouch.* His words are a hard slap across my cheek that wakes me from a trance, leaving my body pulsing and trembling with want. The sting of his rejection, however, is quick to rise, reminding me that he's tainted by life and loss and everything bad in this world. He's stuck in the past, and I need to look forward. If I don't, I'll lose myself again, which means all my yo-yoing is stupid.

"Georgie?" Sam snaps his fingers. "You all right?"

"Ye-yep," I say.

"I hope you understand—about us, I mean."

"Did I ever tell you why I lied about my name and wanted that internship with you?"

"No."

"Because I was tired of being underestimated by everyone, tired of feeling weak and sad. But most of all, because I wanted to be free, and to do that, I had to fight for it—for my voice—so that I could help my family and decide my future instead of my fears deciding it for me." I take a long breath. *I have to get off the hamster wheel with this guy.* I've been through too much, and he's too much temptation. "I really can't be around you anymore. I'll finish helping prove my brother is innocent, but after that, I don't want to see you again."

"Georgie! Dammit!" I hear Abi off in the distance. "Come on!"

"Looks like your friend needs you. You going in?" he says, his voice barren of any emotion.

So, basically, he couldn't care less about never seeing me again. I won't lie, a tiny piece of me hurts—rejection is a sting everyone feels, no matter how strong—but it's the confirmation I needed. *I have to let this go.*

"Yeah. I think I'd like to meet this Mitch. I hear he's something to look at." I wink. "More my age, yanno?"

I walk off and head into the party with Abi.

# CHAPTER TWENTY-ONE

The moment we approach the front door, Mitch steps forward, past the security guard, to greet us.

"I'm sorry about the mix-up, ladies," he says, in the most adorable Australian accent I've ever heard.

"I'm just happy I caught her," Abi says. "She was trying to make a getaway."

"Well, no one gets away from one of my parties until they've had some fun." Mitch dips his head and gestures for us to enter.

We sail inside, and this time, everyone's staring because we're getting very special attention from the man himself. I notice there's a mini version of him—still attractive but shorter and blonder—standing to his side. Must be his cousin because he immediately sweeps Abi away in search of cocktails for us.

"So you must be Georgie," Mitch says.

*Wow.* I get a better look at those eyes, a stunning light hazel. He's also super freaking tall, and though he's wearing an untucked dress shirt and slacks, I can tell right away he's a swimmer slash underwear model; his clothing swells in all the right spots. *Speaking of swells...* Involuntarily, I feel my eyes pulling south. After all, he's got a very special nickname, the Bulge, and I've seen the swimsuit pics. Who knows when I'll ever be this close to such a legendary dick again.

"Sam! Hey, thanks for making it, mate." Mitch gives the old bro hug to Sam, who is now behind me.

*I stand corrected. I'll have plenty more opportunities.* And isn't Sam the least bit concerned that Abi will see him? She still thinks he's Mr. Brooks.

"Said I'd stop by." Sam gives Mitch a fist bump. "Welcome to the States."

"Thanks, mate," Mitch says. "This is a huge move."

"I'm sure you made the right choice, Mitch," Sam says. "And you've got all of us behind you."

Mitch pats Sam's shoulder. "Well, come on in. Bar's that way. Food's that way. Girls are everywhere."

I stand there, feeling invisible at this weird bro-reunion-fest.

"Thanks," says Sam. "I'm not staying long, but I wanted to welcome you to your new home. We're all happy to have you swimming for us."

I'm guessing Mitch will be training here in Houston, maybe at my university since they have a world-class swim team.

"You're the fucking best." Mitch gives Sam one

last man-embrace and heads off to greet the other guests.

"What are you doing?" I whisper to Sam.

"Saying hi to an old friend."

"How do you know him?" I ask.

"Sorry. Can't tell you that."

I roll my eyes. "Fine. Whatever. But Abi is here, *Mr. Brooks.*"

"Then I guess I'll just have to be my rude self so she stays away."

"How about leaving?" I suggest.

"Sorry. I have a job to do. I go when you go." Sam walks off in the other direction.

*Wonderful.* He plans to babysit me—just the exact opposite of what I told him I wanted out of life.

"I'm having fun tonight," I call to the back of his head, "so don't ruin it with your crusty old-man vibe!" I'm unsure if he hears me, but I see his spine straighten and his fist ball as he disappears into the next room.

*Yeah, he heard me.* I smile and go off to find Abi and her friend. It's time to erase Sam from my thoughts and accomplish what I set out to do. Have fun.

It's just after midnight, and I am hammered. It's not a sloppy stumbling drunk that will shame me in the morning, but it's the best buzz of my life. My inhibitions are gone, I'm lucid and in control, and most importantly I'm dancing on a pool table while people are pumping their fists and screaming at me. Abi is in the corner, making out with Mitch of all people, and I couldn't be more fucking happy than I am at this very moment. Right now, I'm not shy, worried, or hiding. I don't feel the weight of my family name, the legal battles, or my past threatening to crush me like a boulder of doom.

I raise my arms in the air and scream as the dance music pounds through my ears. The room of a hundred plus are drunk as shit, laughing and dancing, too.

"Come on, Georgie. That's enough!" I look down and see Sam standing there like my disapproving father.

*What's he still doing here?* "Get lost, geezer!"

He narrows his eyes. "Georgie, you have work to do tomorrow. The fun is over."

I flash my middle fingers in his face. "Bite me, Agent McPartypooper!"

He shakes his head, and no one around us seems to notice a battle of wills is about to go down.

He gestures with his hands for me to get off the table before he loses his patience.

I bend over and wag my drunk-ass finger in his stern face. "You want me? Then you have to kiss me." I stand up and throw my arms in the air. "Anyone! Anyone who wants me! Just has to kiss me!"

I hear several takers and probably a few who are so wasted they'll cheer for anything.

"Georgie, come down. Time to go home," he snarls loudly.

"You gonna kiss me?" I slur. *Okay, maybe I am sloppy wasted. So what?*

"If I do, will you go home?" he asks, pissed as ever.

I shrug just to annoy him. "If it's a good kiss."

"Fine. Come down, and I'll kiss you."

I point in his face. "I kneeeew you wanted me."

He reaches for me, and I stumble and fall into his arms.

"Yeah! Good catch, Agent Fogey." I chuckle and pat his cheek a little too hard. *Oops!*

"Stop it. You're acting childish." He carries me off through a blur of rooms, and suddenly, we're at the front door.

"Heeeeey…where's my kiss?" I hiccup.

"It's waiting for you at home."

"Nope. Nope! That wasn't the deal. Help! He's kidnapping me!" I yell, drawing the attention of several partygoers.

"Shut up, Georgie. You're causing a scene." His eyes are practically shooting angry lightning bolts.

"That's what we do, us young, smart women who can't be playthings." I poke his nose.

"Stop that." Still carrying me, he manages to hand a ticket to the valet and then gives me a stern look.

"Ohhhh...no. Mr. A-hole is giving orders." I clap. "Listen up, everyone, Mr. A-hole here says we should all quit having fun!"

He rolls his eyes. "I swear if you weren't so drunk, I'd spank you," he grumbles under his breath.

I clap again. "Yes. Yes. A good spanking," I say with an English accent, but I'm not sure he gets the Monty Python reference.

His car, a big black SUV, pulls up. He lowers me to my feet, takes my arm, and shoves me inside. "Not a peep, Georgie."

Of course, I'm drunker than hell for my very first time, so there's only one thing for me to do. "Peep! Peep! Peep!"

He gets into the driver's side and tries to ignore my juvenile antics, but I'm not having it. He's harshing on my party vibe. Boo him. In fact, his car is an instant buzz kill, all quiet and lacking dancing.

"It sucks in here. I want to go back." I start reaching for the door handle.

"Georgie!" he yells. "Cut it out, or so help me I will hog-tie you and throw you in the back."

Will he now? Sounds kind of fun.

"Yes, sir, Mr. Grey." I salute him. "Where's the rope?" I turn to see what he's got in the backseat and feel my head slam into a thick, cold wall of sad reality. There's a booster seat.

Suddenly, my drunken stupor isn't so amusing

or fun anymore. I'm just being a moron—a fucking idiot who's kept this man from his daughter tonight because he's busy watching over me.

I face the road.

"Are you going to be sick?" he asks.

"No."

"You don't look well."

I can't say what I'm thinking because it's too dark and too emotional, and God knows I don't do well with any of that. "I'm drunk. I'm sorry."

"It's fine. You're allowed to be twenty-one."

I start to tear up like a blubbering fool. "No. No, it's not. I'm a Walton. We're not allowed to be anything but Waltons. Not even loved or happy."

"Things will look better in the morning, I promise."

"But will it?"

"Of course it will," he replies firmly.

"But I won't ever know what it's like to be just me. I won't ever be free to live and do what I want. They'll always be watching, hating, trying to ruin us."

"That's not true, Georgie."

"Isn't it? Isn't that why you want to destroy my family? Isn't that why you're here with me instead of home with Joy? I bet she misses you. I bet she needs you. But you're stuck babysitting a dumbass rich bitch."

Sam looks straight ahead, his face completely unreadable. "I'm here because I didn't want anything to happen to you, but that doesn't mean you should feel bad. Everyone needs a little fun, you most of all. You've been through a lot."

"Huh! Like you care."

"Why do you think I offered to get you into the party? Or how about making you go to that fund-raiser?"

"To subject me to cruel and unusual groping?"

He flashes a sharp glance my way. "No. I thought having a little fun would make you happy."

*He wanted to make me happy?* "Bullshit. I'm the key to your big plan to make every last person pay for the pain they've caused you, and I know because I'm no different. I want everyone who's ever ridiculed me to burn in hell. And that, my friend, is why I never came out of my shell."

"So you're afraid you'll hurt people?"

"I didn't say that. I just want them to burn in hell. I'm too big of a pussy to hurt anyone." I throw my hands into the air. "Flies, you're all safe with me!"

Sam shakes his head as we hit the highway, and I shrink back into my thoughts—my inebriated, horribly wobbly thoughts. "I really, really liked you, Sam. I didn't even care that you're so old."

"I'm *not* old."

"I've met dirt younger than you. But I didn't care. I said to myself, 'Georgie'—not Sydney, but Georgie—'he doesn't let you get away with it.'"

"With what?" he asks, his eyes glued to the road.

"With my bullshit. Everyone's always accommodated me or felt sorry for little Georgie, who'll never be anything. But you, you wouldn't accept that from me. And now, here I am, not accepting it either." I draw a long, slow breath. "I love you for it, Sam. And I always will. I just wish I was enough for you because I don't want parties. I want you. We could be happy together," I mutter, feeling my eyelids sink and my mind going dark. I have so much to say to this man, but the tequila has finally caught up. "You're hot, Sam. I'd like to have babies with you," I mumble before I drift off. And I'm not sure if I'm dreaming, but I think I hear him chuckle.

Either way, I pass out with a smile on my face.

# CHAPTER TWENTY-TWO

It's morning. My head fucking hurts. I have no clue where I am, but I'm fairly sure I hear a child squealing somewhere in the background.

I crack open one eye and turn my head toward a clock on a nightstand that is neither mine nor familiar. One o'clock? From the daylight shining through the light gray curtains, I know it's p.m. not a.m.

*Jesus. How much did I drink?* I'm praying this pain won't last because, dear God, this is not fair. Shouldn't a first-time drunkard get a pass on the hangover?

I slowly sit up, and once the room stops spinning, I get to my feet. I'm still in my green and black dress from last night—excellent news! But I am most definitely in a man's room. There's very little in the way of decorations, and the furniture is modernist—neutral colors, clean, and masculine.

I rub my neck and press my other hand to my forehead. "Ow, ow, ow…" Memories of last night sift through my mental fog. Okay, there were tequila shots, dancing, more shots, more dancing, some food—I think tacos? Or sandwiches? Hell. I don't remember. Then there was a friendly game of pool, which I lost. I then recall dancing for penance and Sam dragging me home.

*Sam!* I'm in Sam's house. I look around the room. Yes, it even smells like him, all sagey and leathery. *Wait, did I tell him I love him?* My mind scrambles. Oh no. I most definitely did. *Christ, Georgie! What happened to moving forward? To putting him behind you?* I can only hope he'll just forget about the entire thing. Not like I meant it. Especially, the "let's have babies" part.

*Ugh. Boozmiliation.*

I stagger to my feet, stumble to the small all-blue bathroom, and try to rinse the old-sock taste from my mouth. When I look in the mirror, one of my fake eyelashes is stuck to my chin. *Nice. You're a born princess.*

I clean myself up, rinse with Sam's mouthwash, and contemplate using some of his herbal-smelling deodorant. *Ewww...* Hangover and man-stick do not mix.

I grab my heels and purse and quietly open the bedroom door, hoping I can sneak outside and grab a shame-cab home. It's then that I realize I'm not in his apartment. There are family photos all over the hallway.

I lean forward, checking out one of him and a bunch of people on some camping trip.

"Georgie? You up?" The deep manly voice bucks inside my throbbing eardrums.

I cringe, feeling like I've been caught snooping. "Yeah?"

"'Bout time."

I tiptoe for no damned reason—shame, I guess—into what looks like Sam's living room. It's open and warm with a fireplace, comfy khaki couch, plush brown armchair, and a play area with brightly colored blocks in the corner. Sam is sitting on the carpeted floor with a chubby little toddler in pink overalls.

I can't believe how beautiful she is. The gray eyes, just like her daddy, pouty little lips, fat cheeks, and big smile.

"Ohmygod. Aren't you the sweetest little thing?" I go right to her, and she holds up her arms. I pick her up, and I can't even. "How the hell did you end up with such a gorgeous little girl?" I ask him, but I'm looking at this bundle of curls and sweet smiles, who's clearly all energy and wiggles.

"I stole her," he says sarcastically.

"Of course you did," I say in a deep, playful voice. "Becawz there's no way this big ol' ugwy ogre is yo daddy. Now is there, pumpkin?"

She giggles, and I can't explain it, but it's like when you see the most adorable puppy in the world, wagging its tail at you from the store window, and your heart just wants to take it home, cuddle and kiss it to death. Joy is that times a hundred.

"Bo! Bo!" Joy points to the floor toward a fuzzy stuffed boat that has miniature animals shoved inside.

"Oh, you want your boat? Well, the hungover lady says that's a great idea because she just might toss her cookies if she doesn't have some water."

"Water!" Joy barks.

I laugh and set her down.

"It's this way." Sam gets up, and I can see the tension in his shoulders. It puts me on edge.

We enter the kitchen, which is small but cute— white cupboards, brown and white marble counters, and an eating area. O-shaped cereal is scattered across the wooden kitchen table, and a sippy cup of unfinished milk is parked on the high chair.

"I'm sorry about last night," I blurt out. "I swear I've never been drunk, and I promise it will be my last."

With his back to me, he grabs a glass from the cupboard and fills it with tap water from the sink. "Where do you get off doing that?" He turns and shoves the glass at me.

I take it with a hesitant hand. "Doing…what?"

"Joy is not a toy."

I blink at him. "I-I'm so sorry."

"I brought you here because the paparazzi figured out who you are and were following me. I had to drive for over two hours to lose them. We ended up closer to my house than my apartment, and I was falling asleep."

Sam is visibly upset—pulsing jaw, tight lips, dark brows shoved together.

I hold up my hands. "I'm sorry. Really. But I didn't mean any harm by that." I point to the living room, toward Joy. "She's beautiful, Sam. Truly beautiful."

I want to say that her eyes remind me of him and so does her smile, but clearly I've upset him by holding his daughter. I'm not welcome here, and I'm not just talking about his home. I'm not welcome in his life.

"I'll go now," I say.

"Good."

I nod hesitantly. "And thank you for making sure I didn't make too big a fool out of myself last night."

"Don't mention it."

I turn and head through the living room to the front door, ignoring Joy's pleas for me to see her boat again. It feels like a girl-dick move, but Sam's made his feelings clear.

"See you at your apartment tonight?" I ask.

"There's a change of plans. Your brother has an emergency meeting at one of the refineries today at six."

"Tonight?"

"I'll be in front of his building at six thirty. Don't be late."

I'm not ready for whatever comes next, but most of all, I'm thinking that after tonight, Sam will be gone from my life. He'll have what he needs. Henry will be off the hook. I'll be nothing but a job completed, and it breaks my heart.

On the way home, I call Abi and leave her a voice message just to let her know I'm okay. I can only assume she's sleeping off her own headache. Still, I'm dying to hear how it went with "the Bulge."

When I get inside my house, I say hi to my mother, who's playing cards with some friends outside on the terrace—which makes me super happy. I like seeing her trying to get on with her life.

I lie down to take a nap, and when I wake, it's almost six thirty. "Crap!" I shower, throw on a pair of jeans, my red tank, and black flip-flops, and head out. By the time I get to Henry's place, I have seven pissy texts from Sam, and I'm a nervous wreck. But as I walk up to the main building, I realize I'm not frightened by what Sam might find. Henry is so squeaky clean, you could eat off of him. Not that I'd want to because that would be weird. Nevertheless, I'm all jitters and nerves because this is my last encounter with Sam, and if we're really saying goodbye, then I want to tell him that he might be an ogre with a nasty disposition, but to me, he was my knight in shining armor. He changed my life. I want to tell him that I want him to be happy too, and I understand if he doesn't want to be with me, but that I hope he'll find a way to move on—if not for himself, then for his daughter. Because I know what it feels like to be trapped by your thoughts and fears and the scars of your past. But I also know how good it feels to let it all go and to breathe again.

"About time," Sam says when I make my way into the lobby. He's wearing a plain baby blue oxford and jeans that gently hug his masculine thighs. Why does he have to always look so good? It's a distraction to my hormone-saturated body.

"Sorry," I say. "I had to talk to a man about some Gatorade and Tylenol."

"You're hysterical," he says dryly, refusing to remove his mirrored sunglasses.

"Okay then." I go up to the security counter, show them my ID, and away we go into the elevator. The apartment is actually owned by our holdings company, and I'm on Henry's account as a "welcome anytime" family member. His place also has a keypad to enter, so there's no need for a key.

As we're riding up to the penthouse, I can practically see the steam rising from the top of Sam's head of dark hair. I don't know why exactly, but his pissedoffness irritates me.

"Would you stop already?"

Looking ahead, he says, "Don't know what you mean."

"Yes, you do. And for the record, I'm the one who should be mad."

"Why's that?"

"I'm breaking into my own brother's home so you can steal something from his safe."

"If he's got nothing to hide, then there's no problem."

I narrow my eyes at him even though he's not looking at me. "Cut the crap, Agent McDaniel. You know how much I love Henry, and you're making me betray him just to keep him out of jail."

"Life is tough. Get used to it."

The elevator doors chime open, and we step out.

"Well, you're making it a lot harder than it needs to be." I walk past him, go to the keypad, and enter the code. The door pops open, and he sails inside as if it's casual spy-Friday and we're not doing something horribly wrong.

"Bedroom's that way." I point to the right, down the hallway.

Henry and Elle are at some meeting tonight. There's been an issue at one of the oil refineries, and some people got hurt. They want to find out what happened because at plants like those, they have a gazillion safety procedures to prevent injuries.

Sam doesn't waste a moment. Within thirty seconds, he's in Henry's walk-in closet.

"What do you think you'll find?" I ask.

"Proof."

"Of what?"

"Enter in this code, and we'll know for sure."

He holds out a piece of paper.

"Why me?" I cross my arms.

"You own part of the company that owns this apartment."

*Oh. I get it.* I don't need a warrant to go into my own safe, just like I didn't need a warrant to hack my own servers.

I step back. "Well, I'm not opening it—not until you and I talk."

"If you're worried about getting immunity, the answer is yes."

*What the hell?* "Immunity for what? I haven't done anything wrong and you know it."

"You hacked into a bank." He shakes the paper at me. "Now let's get on with this."

"I just want to know what comes next? After you've busted Craigson?"

He looks at me with flat lips and angry eyes. "Fine. If you won't do it, then I will. You can go." He steps around me with the paper and starts punching numbers into the keypad.

"No." I push his hands away. "You're not opening that safe until you answer me."

"Why? Why do you want to know what comes next?"

"Because I'm in love with you," I blurt out. "And if this is the end, if this is the point that you let go of the past and move on, then wonderful. But if your plan is to make revenge your lifelong calling, then I want to know because I need to move on."

My heart is pounding with adrenaline. I can't believe I'm saying all this to him, because it's kind of a shock to me, but it's all true.

He turns his body toward me but looks away, his jaw muscles pulsing. "I told you, Georgie, not to waste your time on assholes like me."

"That is not an answer, Sam! When the fuck is this over? When do you say you have enough? Because for my father, the answer was never, and it drove him mad. And as much as I hoped he'd change, it didn't happen. So all I'm asking is a simple question: Are my feelings for you a mistake?" What I really mean to say is, "*Will you ever love me?*"

I see every muscle in his arms and neck tense up. "You're the best thing to happen to me since Kate died."

I release an exasperated breath. "You're impossible," I mutter. Impossible not to love or want. Impossible to walk away from.

Slowly his gaze meets mine, and then something snaps.

# CHAPTER TWENTY-THREE

*This is happening. Really happening.* Sam and I are tearing off each other's clothes, our mouths locked in a fiery kiss, our hands grabbing and touching, my body aching to get closer. If that kiss at the fundraiser was mind-blowing, this is a thousand times better.

He cups my jaw with his rough hand, angling my head to deepen our kiss. Meanwhile, his other hand is undoing his button flies, and I'm stripping off my jeans and panties.

I break for a moment to jerk my red tank top over my head, leaving me completely naked. My hands waste no time, tearing off the buttons on his light blue shirt, exposing his hard pecs and abs. Somewhere in the back of my mind, I hear a whisper of doubt—*Don't do this, Georgie. He'll only hurt you*—but my body has spoken, and it wants him.

I fall back onto the bed, consumed by his touches and the heat of his skin. All I can think of is him.

I lie back, our mouths locked in a smoldering kiss, his one hand on my breast and the other between my legs, brushing and kneading my c-spot. I rock my pelvis into his palm, aching to relieve the tension, but knowing only one thing will do.

My hands brush over his broad shoulders, down the sides of his strong arms, and find their way to his hard ass. He groans deeply and grinds his stiff shaft between my legs as I pull him toward me, an invitation to enter.

In this moment, I'm not thinking about the fact he'll be my first, or that it might hurt. I'm just thinking about how badly I want him inside me and that if he doesn't fuck me, I might lose my mind.

Our bodies writhe and grind together with shameless abandon, and he slides his hands to mine, pressing my arms over my head but never breaking his punishing kiss. I feel the head of his cock prodding my entrance, and I rock against it, urging him in.

"Are you sure?" he whispers between searing hot kisses.

If he's asking whether or not this is a good idea, then no. I'm not sure. But I am sure about wanting him. Even if it's just once, I want to have him, to know what it feels like to be his, to belong to him and him to me.

"Yes. And I'm on the pill," I whisper back. It was originally for non-sex reasons, but I couldn't be happier that it's about to change.

His demanding kisses begin again, and it feels like nothing exists beyond this exact second of time, where his body covers mine and I'm willing to give him everything.

The heat of his mouth and tongue feel hotter with every movement of his silky lips, and the aching need between my legs is unbearable. I grip his ass and pull him into me. Sam obliges with a smooth, powerful thrust that steals my breath. I gasp, breaking the kiss, and tilt my head back.

I feel his body go rigid, though he's deep inside me. "Jesus, Georgie. Really?"

I didn't warn him that this is my first time, but this isn't that kind of sex. It's not well thought out. It's just an act of primal need.

"If you value your life, you won't stop," I say with my eyes shut, doing my absolute best to ignore the sting. The fact is, having Sam, all of him, is better than anything I've ever felt despite the pain.

"I won't stop if you don't want me to," he says tenderly.

We lock eyes, and it feels like he's staring into my soul. Suddenly, I feel like crying. I don't ever want to lose him. Yet this connection only adds fuel to my sinful fire. Is it possible to want a man this much? Because I do.

"Don't stop," I say.

A moment passes before he's back to my lips, slowly pumping his cock into me at first. But as our bodies take over, our pace quickens and he fucks me hard, his back and ass unrelenting as he drives deeper and pushes me closer.

I know I should wait and savor this moment, but the wave crawls through me, radiating from my core, and it's unstoppable.

"Oh God." The orgasm crashes into me like ten thousand tons of pure soul-shattering euphoria. I dig my fingernails into his shoulders, too blinded by the ecstasy to think or speak or want anything but him filling me with every hard inch. I just want him.

"Fuck, Georgie. I can't stop. You feel so good." I feel his body go rigid, and his pelvis slams into me, pushing his cock to the mouth of my womb as he comes. His groan is deep and animalistic, triggering another mind-blowing contraction. There's just something about the sound of his voice that's so sexual and raw—I can't get enough. I'm addicted to it. To him.

I finish with him, every muscle inside my core throbbing and wanting to draw in every drop.

After several long moments, he presses his lips against the crook of my neck, leaving his shaft inside as it twitches out every last euphoric spasm.

I say nothing about how good it feels, about how good he feels, because somewhere deep inside I know this feels right. I say nothing because the bliss of this moment is fading fast and I'm afraid. This meant everything to me. But what did it mean to him?

Panting, he doesn't separate our bodies, and I can't say I want him to. I don't want it to end.

"Why didn't you tell me?" he whispers against my neck.

He's talking about the fact I was a virgin. "Would it have stopped you?"

"No."

I inhale and release. "Good."

"Georgie?" I hear a soft voice say from a few feet away. I lift my head to find Elle standing with wide eyes. "What the hell are you doing?"

Henry's towering frame appears right behind her, and the look on his face is pure shock. In that moment, I think Sam realizes, as do I, that we have in fact just been fucking in their bed.

Sam gets to his feet and grabs his jeans, holding them to his groin.

I dash for my clothes, too, muttering something incoherent.

"I'm going to fucking kill you," Henry snarls.

I turn my head and follow the hateful beam shooting from Henry's eyes toward his white comforter.

A bright red spot. *Oh, God. Now that's embarrassing.*

"You fucked my baby sister! You fucking took her virginity in my bed!" Henry roars.

*Ooohhh…*I wince. It sounds so much worse spoken aloud. By my brother.

"Henry!" Elle jumps in front of Henry to halt

what will surely be a horrific murder. Because as big as Sam and his muscles are, Henry is at least fifty pounds heavier and built like an armored tank.

"Go!" I tell Sam, sweeping the comforter to the floor and wrapping the sheet around my body.

There's a hesitation in Sam's eyes, and I can tell leaving me is not what he wants. Or maybe he's simply conflicted because he feels something for me, like I do for him, but he's not ready to let go of what was done to his wife. Either way, he's about to have his body broken into many pieces if he doesn't leave.

"I'll call you later." I nod, urging him to go.

He looks at Henry and then at me before cupping my jaw. The kiss is quick, but it means the world to me. I've finally broken through that cold heart. And I know that this thing between us isn't nothing, though I'm unsure how this could possibly work out. He's a single dad with a broken heart. And I'm a young woman figuring out how to find my place in this world. The one thing we have in common is that we're both trying to be happy. I think.

# CHAPTER TWENTY-FOUR

"Explain it again, Georgie," my brother growls from the armchair across from me, "because I'm somehow missing the point where working with the FBI, to have me and my wife convicted, makes one fuck of sense!"

Now dressed and sitting on Henry's couch, I look up at Elle, who shoves a cup of tea at me. A splash of warm liquid dribbles down the front of my red tank top.

*Oh boy. She's pissed.* I have to make them understand.

"He said," I explain once again, "that he doesn't believe you're involved, so he offered me a choice: Help him gather evidence that might prove your innocence, or don't help him and you both get arrested."

Henry stands and starts pacing. "You should've come to me, Georgie. You should've told me."

"So you could do what?" I ask.

Elle chimes in, "That's not the point."

"Then what is?" I ask. "Because it was the only

way to protect you guys."

Henry shakes his finger at me. "We would have figured it out. Together. As a family, Georgie. Instead, you trusted that..." He throws his arms into the air. "That sexual predator."

"Whoa. Hold on," I say. "If there was any predating—or predatorying—or whatever!—it was all me. And I'll remind you that I'm a grown woman."

"He's using you to get to us!" Henry yells.

Okay. They've already made up their minds about Sam. And though I can't blame them, I know they're wrong.

I inhale slowly. "I know what this looks like, but—"

"No buts, Georgie!" Henry bellows. "He manipulated you to get into my safe. He used you."

I look up at Henry. "But you have nothing to hide, right?"

"There's nothing in the safe except a few watches and my passport." Henry's voice is suspiciously edgy.

*Hold on.* "That wasn't my question. You don't have anything to hide, right?"

He looks away and hisses out a breath.

"Henry?" The fear in Elle's voice is pronounced.

"I knew." Henry shakes his head. "I knew what they were doing at PVP."

My blood suddenly feels ice cold. "What?"

"Please tell me you're joking, Henry." Elle covers her mouth.

"I found out a few weeks after my family was presumed dead and you and I took over the companies." Henry's eyes turn glossy.

"Then why didn't you do anything?" Elle, too, is on the brink of tears. "My mother has cancer. How the *fuck* could you deprive anyone of a chance to live, when you know what I've been going through?"

"My father is a greedy asshole," Henry says with a resentful quake in his voice. "And when I took over, when we thought he died, I knew I couldn't change what he'd done. I could only try to save the ten thousand jobs and families dependent on Walton Holdings."

"That's no excuse, Henry." Elle balls her fists. "People's lives depend on those drugs."

"I know." He bobs his head. "But I had to choose my battles, and if I fired everyone running PVP, then everything would've ground to a halt. The manufacturing processes are all proprietary and on lockdown. Not even the production teams know the full formulas. It's all handled in complete secrecy by a handful of people all approved by Dad. He decided who got access to what so they could control the market. They're like the fucking cancer-drug mafia."

*Oh.* I finally understand. Henry had to choose between saving a few or saving no one.

He continues, "I hoped over time Craigson would trust me and we'd get what we needed to remove the stranglehold. But until then, I had to let them continue their fucking bullshit or risk losing the drugs."

I don't know much about pharmaceuticals, but if PVP has all of their trade secrets locked up, Henry's right. We could lose those lifesaving medicines forever.

Henry looks at Elle; his torment is obvious. "I just couldn't do that to you, honey. Your mom needs her medicines."

Elle's eyes tear. "I'm so sorry, Henry. But you should've told me."

"What could you possibly do?" he asks her.

Elle sighs. "I don't have a fucking clue, but we would have figured it out together."

"So." I stand from the couch. "Seems we all decided to play the lone-hero idiots when we should've been trying to figure this out together." And sadly, this is the kind of impossible situation we all feared. If word gets out, it will be the ammo our enemies need to break up Walton Holdings. At this point, however, I'm not sure I care. We're fighting to keep my dad's empire alive, and if we succeed, we'll only be faced with challenge after challenge. Someone will always be lurking in the shadows, hoping to take us out. It's the way of the world. Only now, we have the fuckers at PVP who hold the key to thousands of lives. They can burn it all to the ground if we misstep.

Elle shakes her head. "I've solved thousands of

problems of every sort imaginable, and I don't have a solution."

Henry grabs her hand. "You're still the smartest woman on the planet—the smartest human, I mean."

"Glad you added that part." She takes his hand and kisses his palm.

I can't help wanting that sort of undying love for myself. It's unconditional and touching. Yet, oddly, I feel sorry for them. They'll never be free to live normal happy lives if we stay on this path.

"I have an idea," I say. "We put everything up for sale."

Elle and Henry look at me like I'm mad.

"The whole enchilada," I explain. "Every single company so the PVP guys don't suspect anything. And we make part of the deal a generous buyout of the PVP executives contingent upon a successful transfer of all intellectual property," I add.

"Who are you, and what have you done with my quiet, timid little sister?" Henry smiles proudly.

Elle blinks. "The only problem is that we need a credible buyer."

"What if we make one up?" I say. "A private shell company. We'll pull out of it once we, the owners, have what we need to run PVP on our own."

Henry smiles. "I actually think it's a good idea, Georgie."

"FBI! Down on the ground!" Deep voices boom

through Henry's penthouse. It only takes a moment to realize that Sam betrayed me. He needed revenge more than he needed my love.

# CHAPTER TWENTY-FIVE

"You okay?" says Mr. Palmer, a lawyer from the new firm we hired to handle the battle with my father. I never met the man before today, but he looks like the type of well-seasoned person who knows how to play hardball—deep frown lines, white hair, and an expensive suit. He got me out on bail and miraculously arranged to have me escorted out the back, escaping the eyes of the media.

"Am I okay?" I ask, debating if now would be a good time for a stress cry. "Hmmm...I was arrested, handcuffed, and had to share a cell with a woman named Mitsy, who had an X-rated Hello Kitty tattoo on her forehead. So I'm fanfuckingtastic."

"Just be thankful you have the resources to help you fight."

He's right. But I still can't believe everything that's happened, and I'm unsure which part is harder to swallow—that I actually have a record now, that from this day forward everyone will know who I am, or that Sam did this to me only hours after taking my virginity. Okay. Yes, I gave it to him, but it's too awful for words.

I slide into the back of a waiting sedan. It's eight in the morning, and I know Palmer is still working to get Elle and Henry out, too. My mother is with Claire and Michelle, who were not arrested since none of them ever ran the holdings company or were directly involved with PVP, but it's a moot point. The FBI arrested Craigson and everyone else in charge at PVP, too. My guess is that Sam had no clue that doing so would immediately stop all production.

*Goddammit, Sam.* Why in the world would he do this to me? I'm beyond devastated, but there's no time to sulk or sob or think of myself. I have to focus on people like Elle's mother and get those drugs back in production.

"Take me to see my dad," I say to Palmer once he's in the car, sitting beside me.

"I don't advise having contact with him. People could get the impression you're up to something, which might undermine our defense."

"Thanks for the warning, but seeing him is more important." Though my thoughts are with Palmer, not wanting to have anything to do with my father.

An hour later I'm sitting in a Plexiglas booth at the state prison just outside Houston. It's quite possibly the saddest place I've ever been with its barbed-wire fences and gray cement stucco. The registration room is windowless, cold, and smells of depression. When I'm finally called, they take me through a steel bar gate into another room where correctional officers stand on both sides of the glass. I hate what my father did to us. Truly I do. But there's a part of my heart that hurts for him. This is an awful place. Definitely not good for naked yoga either.

Wearing an orange jumpsuit, my dad sits and picks up the white phone. He's a large man like Henry, but with a blond crew cut and a perma-snarl.

"I wasn't expecting to see you here," he says.

I'm about to get straight to the point, but I freeze up. My brain is overwhelmed with so many emotions, starting with the hurt I feel over him belittling me my entire life; almost killing me, my mother, and sisters; and every other selfish, cruel act that shows how little he cares about us and the human race in general. I want to tell him how I'm unsure I'll ever be completely okay because of it. But mostly, I want to tell him how sorry I feel for him because he has an amazing family who would've made him happy had he bothered to love us as much as his money. Sadly, I can't say these things. I can only stare with revulsion.

"You always were a disappointing conversation-alist," he says.

"We-well," I eek out, "things have cha-changed."

"Really now?" He shakes his head.

"Ye-yes."

"Then why do you look like the same old timid little Georgie who pisses herself when anyone looks her in the eyes?"

"You're a monster," I whisper into the phone.

He chuckles and leans in. "I'm also a goddamned genius. One who always gets what he wants."

Is that how he sees himself? *Pathetic.*

"So what *do* you want?" I mutter. "Because I'd love to know."

"What any man wants: To enjoy the fruits of his labor. To have a legacy."

"So that means…?"

His eyes shift from side to side, checking to see who's listening. He *must* be bonkers because there's no such thing as privacy when you're in jail.

*But those guards aren't the ones he should be worried about.* That person is sitting right here in front of him, and she's finally figured out that being underestimated is her weapon.

"It means," he winks, "that I am always ten steps ahead. Don't you ever doubt it, Georgie. Daddy knows what he's doing."

I lean away from the glass, wondering if this is all some scam. *Of course. The insanity plea could only work if he did something truly insane.* Like kidnapping your own family and starting a naked yoga cult. He's likely going to avoid any real jail time for kidnapping us, and the FBI hasn't bothered him with any of this pharmaceutical bullshit. Why would they when he's already locked up and only going to plead insanity? For the moment, they have bigger fish to fry.

"This was your plan all along," I conclude.

He shrugs. "Maybe I knew something you didn't. Maybe I did what was needed to ensure I live to fight another day and keep my empire intact with the right people by my side."

*He knew.* He knew the FBI was onto him and PVP. I can't help jumping to the absolute darkest thought possible. *He took us away and left Henry behind to be in charge.* Henry, the son he couldn't tame or control.

"You set up Henry to take the blame, didn't you?"

My father flashes a sinister smile that touches his eyes, and I'm suddenly ashamed of every one of my body parts that looks like him, right down to my green irises. He seems all too happy that Henry is taking the fall, which only confirms my suspicions: my dad has no soul. He loves no one but himself. Which is why Henry never wanted anything to do with him or the company. He just wanted to play football, which my father was staunchly opposed to. I'm guessing Henry's rejection of the whole Chester Empire made Henry disposable. *And the ideal scapegoat for my father's actions.*

The rage starts to bubble over. Henry is the nicest, most honorable man I've ever met. Elle is the sort of woman—strong, compassionate, and intelligent—that people like me look up to. But to a greedy pig like my father, they're fodder for his greed machine.

I clear my throat, finding myself and my voice. "Well, Dad, I have some very bad news for you. We've decided to sell it all off. Every oil field, every production plant, every company. Mom, Michelle, Claire, and I have decided that we don't want anything to do with Walton Holdings. Or you. So whatever plan you had is over."

He narrows his green eyes. "You're not so good at bluffing, Georgie. I can see right through you."

"You think I'm bluffing? I'm not. Because the moment I walk out of here, I'm going straight to the press. I'll go to any network who'll hear me that my father almost killed his own family just to convince a judge that he's insane because the FBI found out he was selling lifesaving drugs to the highest bidders on the black market. And instead of taking the blame, he set up his own son to take the fall. Hell, maybe my dad even worked out a deal with Craigson to testify against Henry in exchange for a tidy sum. Because we all know the money on PVP's books was just the tip of the iceberg. There has to be billions more because it's the only way so many executives would do something so heinous to dying people—mothers, fathers, daughters, and sons. And when that gets out, which I will ensure it does, there isn't a soul on this planet who will believe you're insane, because it's just too damned evil and complicated." I slap my hand on the counter. "So I'll ask you once, Dad. Where are all of the PVP formulations kept?"

He bobs his head approvingly. "I'm proud, Georgie. You've finally grown some balls. Maybe you'll amount to something someday."

I can't believe this man is my father.

"So," he continues, "what do I get if I tell you?"

"What do you want?" *Besides a painless death when I'm done with you, which you won't get.* Prison cafeteria shit-on-a-shingle and E. coli-covered romaine are the best he can hope for if I have any input. *I might even throw in Mitsy.*

"You need to testify at my hearing and do what my lawyers say. Down to the letter."

*Ohellno.* I'll tell the truth. I'll tell the world about Sam's wife and his now motherless daughter. I'll tell everyone about the crazy BS my father did to cover his ass. I don't care if I'm digging my own grave because I'm a Walton, too, and our wagons are hitched by name and blood. This can't go on.

"So," I say with a timid voice I'm actually faking this time, "you want me to convince a judge you're crazy."

"Whatever my lawyers tell you to do."

"And the holdings company?" *Dig that hole, Dad. Come on.*

"Once you all sign a contract relinquishing your rights to sell Walton Holdings, then I will give you what you need for your humanitarian, bleeding-heart bullshit."

"We can't wait that long, Dad. And I don't think I can convince Michelle and Claire to agree to your deal unless you prove we can trust you. You almost killed us, and the pilot died. Then you held us prisoner and threatened to marry us off to some naked beach bums." Of course, I mean "bum" in the butt sense.

"No one died, Georgie," my father says dismissively with a flick of his wrist. "The pilot was rescued hours before we were, and the cult members were just well-paid actors. I would never allow such inbred scum to touch a Walton."

I look up and my mouth falls open. "Wow. You are worse than a raging case of herpes. That has crabs and tapeworms as best friends."

"Very descriptive, Georgie, but do we have a deal?"

"Where's the PVP stuff kept?" It can't be somewhere too crazy because the VP of manufacturing has to have access to everything on a fairly regular basis.

"The server for Algae-Tech."

Of course. No one would think to look for it at another unrelated company.

"Thanks, Dad. You've taken the first step to saving your soul. Sadly, I can't help you with the rest of your pathetic, shitty, shallow life. But I'll always love you. Not because you deserve it, but because I'm a damned good person who prefers that over hating you."

I stand and pull my earpiece and mic from behind my ear, which I had covered up with my long hair and threaded under my shirt. I tuck the wire into my pocket, where my cell phone has been recording every word. Like I said, always being underestimated can sometimes work to one's advantage, and today, it saved my family.

"You fucking little bitch," he growls.

"Goodbye, Dad." I turn and leave, hearing the sounds of him attacking the glass and guards yelling.

I could say I feel vindicated in some small way, but there's nothing but pain in my heart. I had hoped to hear a denial or rational explanation for this fucked-up, callous crap. Instead he exceeded my worst suspicions. Not only had he orchestrated the plane crash, but he constricted the supply of a drug that could help a lot of people.

*He's a monster.* I slide into the black sedan waiting in the prison parking lot with Palmer.

"You get what you need, Miss Walton?"

I nod. "Sadly, yes." Though, I'll wait for the right time to hand over the recording. I have a feeling my family will need the leverage.

"Sometimes we have to make choices." He pats my hand. "And we've got to take comfort in the fact we've done our best."

I've never heard truer words. "You're right. And now I have work to do, starting with you telling me how to make sure my father goes to a real prison for a long time along with the PVP executives who helped him."

Palmer's phone rings. "Hello?" He listens intently and nods his head. "Excellent news. I'll let her know." He ends the call and looks at me. "The FBI wants to make a deal."

"Good. Because so do I."

# CHAPTER TWENTY-SIX

Though I am dreading seeing Sam again, I'm also eager to get this over with, so the two days it takes for Palmer to set up the meeting with the FBI is torture.

Elle has been let out on bail, but Henry was considered a flight risk due to his potential access to cash.

*Ridiculous that he'd leave the country. He would never abandon us.* Sadly, he's Chester Walton's son, so people automatically assume the worst.

The good news is that today might be the turning point if it goes right. Elle and I have agreed to an interview that could result in a favorable plea bargain or charges being dropped. I'm hoping for the latter because I've done nothing wrong, though Palmer says I'm leverage against Henry. If we don't reach a deal today, then they'll likely pressure Henry to take the blame in exchange for me and Elle going free.

I'm not having it.

The other news is that we found the PVP formulas, and the wheels are in motion as we speak to get production moving. Elle's made sure, as have the lawyers, that the people put in charge will run product until all demand has been met. Our salespeople will charge the minimum price possible starting immediately. Still, those are just Band-Aids. Word has gotten out about the scandal, and the public is in an uproar. My family is officially one of the most hated in the world. "Cancer patient killers," "The demons of death," "America's biggest billionaire buttheads." That last one came from this morning's tabloid.

We walk into a large conference room situated downtown at the bureau's satellite office. Both in suits and blouses, Elle and I sit together. Our five meanest-looking lawyers on the planet, including Palmer, sit on either side of us. With this much legal action flanking me, I feel like a big-time criminal. Or a butthead. Either-or.

As we wait, my blood pressure spikes, and I can't help squirming in the hard plastic chair. I'm moments away from seeing the man who's broken my heart, systematically lied to me, and who slept with me while stabbing me in the back. I've never met a crueler person, besides my father, but at least good old Dad never hid what he was. Sam went out of his way to make me trust him.

*Did he, though?* Sam repeatedly said he was an asshole. Then I repeatedly ignored him. Honestly, I have no one to blame but Georgie Walton. I dug myself into this hole. *And now I'm going to dig myself out.*

The door opens and in walk two gentlemen in white shirts and blue ties, whom I've never seen before. *No Sam?*

The men sit, Palmer greets them, and I instantly get the feeling this isn't going to go well. Elle senses it too because she reaches under the table for my hand and holds it.

"Thank you for coming," says the shorter man, with dark hair and glasses, sitting on the right. "I'm Agent Wilson. This is Agent Peekles."

*Peekles?* I snicker. I can't help it. "Sorry. Nerves."

Wilson frowns and continues, "As you're aware, very serious charges have been brought against your clients, Mr. Palmer."

*I guess you could say we're in a...peekle?* I try not to laugh. The stress is definitely getting to me, but at least I'm not turning green. *Just a case of the giggles. I mean peekles.*

He continues, "Our purpose here today is to interview your clients and determine if a plea can be reached. Of course, we're only willing to offer one if we're convinced that they can be of use in convicting Chester Walton, Henry Walton, and the eight Palo Verde Pharmaceuticals executives, all under indictment for the illegal sale of regulated substances, violating ten antitrust—"

"Excuse me," I say, "but where's Agent McDaniel?"

Wilson and Peekles—*oh, God. How is that his name?*—exchange glances, but Wilson speaks up. "Agent McDaniel resigned. He is no longer with the bureau."

*He quit?* "Since when?"

Wilson's beady brown eyes flicker. "We are not at liberty to discuss that, nor are we here to do so. This meeting is to determine—"

"Yeah," I cut in, no longer laughing, "but this was Sam's investigation. It was important to him." For Sam to dump his job when he was so close to vindication doesn't make sense. I mean, this man went undercover for six months. He literally wore the "meanest boss in the world hat" as a cover.

My heart quickly wants to believe he left because of me and that he had nothing to do with our arrests, but my mind kicks me in the backside and reminds me how trusting him in the past hasn't turned out so awesome.

"Like I said, I'm not at liberty to discuss Sam McDaniel," Wilson says.

My mind reels with speculation. Sam said he thought Elle and Henry were innocent. He certainly didn't believe I had anything to do with this PVP mess. Otherwise, he wouldn't have touched me. Not when his wife died because of all this. Yet he slept with me. And then I was arrested, but they never found a thing, did they? And maybe they got into Henry's safe. Maybe they didn't. But Henry said there wasn't anything in there.

*I'm guessing they've got nothing because there is nothing.* They can only go after Henry and Elle because they were in charge, but that's not really evidence of wrongdoing. And now their only hope is to back Elle or me into a corner and get a plea with our agreement to help convict my brother, Dad, and the PVP executives. Well, I'm all for punishing the real culprits, but not at the expense of falsely accusing Henry. Or by admitting to a crime I didn't commit.

"I'm sorry." I stand up. "This was a mistake."

"Miss Walton, where are you going?" Palmer asks, his hard blue eyes warning me not to do anything rash.

"These gentlemen are wasting our time." I look at the faces across the table. "You don't have anything on Henry, Elle, or me because we haven't done anything. In fact, I think that's why Sam quit. When you came up empty-handed, you insisted on arresting us based on an assumption, but now the clock is ticking and you're going to have to drop all the charges unless *we* give you something. Well, we won't."

The two men don't blink.

"Miss Walton," says Palmer, "as your attorney, I strongly recommend you cease talking and we reconvene—"

"That won't be necessary," I crinkle my nose, "because I'm guessing if I call Sam right now, he'll tell me I'm right. Isn't that so, gentlemen?"

They say nothing, but their snarling faces are a dead giveaway. I'm right.

"See. You all know we had nothing to do with what those pigs were up to. But I can tell you this: we are willing to help, but not at the price you're offering. So if you want Chester Walton, I can give him to you. I can testify about what he told me when I went to see him the other day—the fake insanity, the plan to have Henry take the blame. I may even have made a recording you can use. But you'll get nothing from me unless you drop all the charges against the three of us." I smile. "This witch hunt is over."

I turn and walk out. Elle catches up to me quickly. "Jesus, Georgie. What was that?"

"I'm right. I know I am."

"I sure hope so because this is our lives we're talking about."

Sam would never quit when he was so close unless he had a reason. All he wanted was justice for his poor wife. He didn't want to hurt me or put me in jail. "I've never been surer about anything in my entire life."

"Who are you?" Elle says with a smile. "And where have you put our little Georgie?"

I push the elevator call button. "She grew up."

જે જી

As I'm on my way to Sam's house, my cell phone starts buzzing and ringing off the hook. I hit the button on my steering wheel, praying that I didn't make a mistake back there. "Hello?"

"Henry is out!" Elle tells me. "Charges against the three of us have been dropped. And I just spoke to Palmer; he told me they'll be setting up another meeting with the FBI to interview you and Henry. To support their case against your dad, of course."

I let out a sigh of relief. "Well, they're not getting squat until they issue a statement clearing all our names."

"Good thinking," Elle says. "Hey, you really should get your law degree. You were a pistol today, Georgie."

*I kinda was, wasn't I?* Oddly, it was almost the same feeling I had when I first stood up to Sam. "Injustice and assholes seem to be the magic antidote for my shyness."

"Where are you now?" she asks.

"I have something to take care of."

"Is it removing the stain from my comforter?" she asks.

I wince. "I'm so sorry about that. Please just burn it, and I'll buy you a new one."

She laughs. "It's no big deal, but I think Henry will want to burn the bed. He'll never be able to achieve an erection in it again."

"Elle! TMI! He's my brother, remember?"

"Oops. Sorry. I keep forgetting that you're not

just a friend, but my sister-in-law, too."

My eyes tear up. Her friend? I admire Elle so much, and the fact she thinks of me like that is humbling.

"Georgie?" she says.

"Yep?" I sniffle.

"Are you crying?"

"Nope." I sob.

"Oh, honey. What's wrong?" she asks.

"Nothing. I'm just—I just really love you guys, that's all. And I'm so happy we're all a family."

"Awww…me too, Georgie. And lucky us, our family will be all together when the baby's due in December."

*Baby.* I can't wait to see it, hold it, love it. I never knew I was a baby person, but I'm beyond excited.

My mind drifts to Sam and Joy. "Do you think there's room for more?"

"Ohmygod," Elle says. "Are you pregnant, too?"

"No. I'm—I've found the man I want to be with."

"Oh, I'm so happy for you, Georgie."

"Thank you." All I have to do now is make sure he wants to be with me.

# CHAPTER TWENTY-SEVEN

As I knock on Sam's front door, a million things are running through my mind. Never in a gazillion years would I have imagined that I'd be the one pursuing this man, a man who once terrified me. Now the only thing that terrifies me is not having him in my life.

The door opens and a pair of silvery eyes greet me. His stubble is extra thick and dark. His face looks tired, like he hasn't slept. Yet, he's more beautiful than ever.

"Hi," I say.

"What are you doing here, Georgie?"

"Can I come in?"

He stares down at me for a long intense moment, but ultimately steps aside.

I enter and immediately notice the house is quiet. "Where's Joy?"

"At the park with my sister-in-law."

"I've met Erin. She's nice."

"When?" he asks.

"It's a long story." I sit on his overstuffed khaki

couch, and my ass is greeted with a squeak. I reach under and pull out a googly-eyed stuffed squirrel. *Warrior squirrel?*

"It's Miss Nutso," Sam says. "Joy's favorite."

*Of course it is.* I smile and set the squirrel on the coffee table. "That reminds me, I brought something for you." I reach into my bag and pull out my light gray teddy bear. It's the kind with an oversized head and a stoic smile. It's a serious teddy bear, meant only for the most serious of conversations and situations.

"You got me a used teddy bear?" Still standing, he takes it reluctantly.

"Oh, that's not used. That's years of love and tears and several cycles through the wash." I shrug. "Because people snot a lot when they cry. But Teddy held up, and now he's yours."

Sam sets the bear on the table beside Miss Nutso and folds his arms over his chest. "Georgie, what do you want?"

"I was thinking how hard it must be, carrying all of your emotions bottled up inside. I used to do it, too, and I know what it feels like, so I thought you might need a friend." I glance at the bear. "Besides, I'm done with him. I prefer people now. The conversations are a bit more satisfying—no offense, Teddy."

"I'm thirty-one, Georgie. I'm perfectly capable of handling my life like a grown man."

"Thirty-one? Jesus, you *are* old." Of course, I'm

only kidding, and he looks so damned good, he could easily pass for late twenties. Nevertheless, I need to make a point.

He narrows his eyes. "I'm *not* old."

"Nope. You're super old. And stubborn. And strong, sexy, frustratingly loyal, and passionate. And you're deep." I nod. "Yeah. I think that's what I like most about you. At first I thought it was bitterness in your eyes, but now I know you have the eyes of a man who's seen a lot. He's been through everything horrible this world has to offer." Like war, the death of his wife, being left to raise a little girl when his heart is filled with anger. "So I'm here, sitting on your couch, offering you a do-over. You can have a new life and fresh start. With me. You'll see what it's like to have nothing but good things waiting for you. Or..." I look at Teddy. "You can have him because you won't let go of the past and choose to keep it all bottled up. He's very absorbent," I add. "Holds lots of tears and snot."

"So," Sam says, his face nothing but hard, cold planes, looking the part of the tough ex-Marine, "you're saying my choices are to date a naïve, twenty-one-year-old college student who doesn't know the first thing about the fucked-up world we live in because she only knows a life of privilege, or...I can choose a snotty, ratty stuffed animal."

"Teddy is clean. But, yes. Minus the naïve part. And the part where you said I don't know anything. Because I do. I've merely chosen to let the bad stuff go and focus on the joy of being alive despite my father almost killing me, the FBI having me and my family arrested, and feeling like I didn't matter and never would for the first twenty-one years of my life." I shrug. "Other than that, though, I'm a fucking catch."

"That was an excellent sales pitch, Georgie. But you forgot one key point."

"What?" I ask.

"You're supposed to start with the bad stuff first, just like I taught you. You were supposed to say that you'll never forgive me for running out on you after we had sex. You were supposed to say that you'll never forgive me for not warning you that they were coming to arrest you."

"That's the bad part, so what's the good news?" He told me once that a good sales pitch saves the best for last.

"The good news is that I resigned two minutes after I left Henry's apartment when my director told me what they planned to do since I came up empty-handed. Then I made it clear I would testify on your behalf—and on Elle's and Henry's too—if they went after you."

*He did that? For us?* It does explain why everything happened so fast today after the meeting. They already knew they couldn't win, just as I suspected. What I hadn't known was that Sam had been pushing behind the scenes to make sure I'd be okay, and he did it at the expense of everything he's spent years working for.

*He protected me.* "I-I don't know what to say."

Still standing on the other side of the coffee table, Sam's posture softens. He looks up at the ceiling and inhales, like he's summoning courage.

Finally, he looks at me with those piercing eyes. "When Kate died, I hid my pain for the sake of Joy, and I believed I would never stop feeling so angry. But then I met you and saw how brave you were. You faced every bit of pain head-on and you didn't give up, not even when I was the biggest asshole in the world to you. You kept going and fighting for yourself, and I think because of that, you made me want to fight, too."

My eyes tear, and I find myself unable to speak. There's just too much emotion in my heart, hearing Sam's confession. I've never seen him so vulnerable, yet all I see is his strength. He's speaking from his heart, and for a man like him, I know it's not easy.

He continues, "So the good news of my sales pitch isn't for you, but for me. Because the moment you were arrested, I thought you'd never forgive me. And then, suddenly, living for revenge didn't make sense anymore. All I could think about was you—how I'd lost you because I fucked up. If only I had let go of my fucking anger, I could've saved you from all that. I would've been able to work something out with the FBI a long time ago." He rubs his bristly chin. "But by some miracle, here you are, asking *me* to be a part of *your* life, and that's better than good news. It's a goddamned miracle." He takes a breath. "Because I admire you, Georgie. I desire you, too. But most of all, I love you."

My heart starts beating a million miles an hour, and I feel light-headed. He gave up years of work and his job to help me. He fought even when he thought I'd never want to see him again.

*Wow.* I had come here today expecting to profess my love and beg him to take one step forward with me. Instead, he tells me he loves me more than revenge, more than his hate. Which, frankly, says a whole hell of a lot.

*I think that good news was for me.* Because while Sam might not be all soft edges and tenderness, he is the sort of man who will always believe in me, and now I know he'll always fight for me, too. Simply put, there is nothing sexier in this world than a guy like that. *Ohmygod. I so love him.*

Still seated on his khaki couch, I gaze up into those emotionally charged eyes and lift my shoulders.

"Did you just shrug?" he asks. "After I tell you I love you, that's your response?"

I shrug again, trying to hold back a smile. It doesn't work.

"You know I hate it when you shrug."

"Do you?" I shrug.

He licks his lips. "Yeah."

"What are you going to do about it?" Shrug, shrug.

He steps around the coffee table. "Wanna find out? I dare you to shrug one more time."

I look up at him with a wicked little grin. Shrug.

He grabs my wrist, yanks me to my feet, and throws me over his shoulder. "You're not drunk this time, so spanking is fair game."

"Oh. A spanking! A spanking," I say in my best British accent, laughing.

He carries me into his bedroom and sets me on my feet, next to the bed. "You know I'd never hit you."

"Dammit! I was kind of hoping." I crack a smile.

"You're really into that?"

"Nah. I think I've taken enough beatings. I'm really ready for a pain-free life." My smile melts away. "I really just want to move on. And I really, really want to do it with you. And Joy—I mean, I know that I'm no substitute for her mother, but I think I could be a positive influence in her life." At the very least, I know what not to do when it comes to children. My father taught me well. "We all deserve a fresh start. I think we need it."

As Sam stares down at me, I see the emotion stirring behind those light gray eyes. Funny, I once thought they were lifeless. Now all I see is life. My life.

"I still don't get why the hell you'd want me after everything that's happened," he says.

"Because I love you," I say quietly.

He slides his hand to the nape of my neck. "You're making it really difficult to say yes to that teddy bear."

"What if I said you could have us both?"

He smiles. "Then I'd have to say it's an offer I can't refuse."

His mouth covers mine, and the heat spikes through my body. I lean into him, savoring his silky lips and the feel of his strong body pressed to mine. The pulses and sinful aches explode like a bomb, crashing through me. I want him. I want him so badly it hurts.

I pull back and whip off my shirt. Next I kick off my heels and start removing my pants. Meanwhile, he's stripping like a man whose clothes are on fire. It takes us a handful of seconds to get naked and for our mouths to be reunited in a fiery kiss that burns through me. He guides me back onto the bed, where he settles between my thighs. His hard, hot body feels delicious against my soft curves.

His wild kiss slows, and then he pulls back his head to stare into my eyes. "Tell me what you want. You're in charge now."

Yes! Little old me is finally having my day! "I think I'd like to hear you say you love me again. And then I'd like us to be happy until we're old and gray. Though you'll get there faster than me, but you get the—"

"Never mind. I'll take the lead." His mouth is

relentless as he kisses me with everything he's got. His hands roam and massage and glide over my taut nipples like he's memorizing every curve within reach. My hands float over the smooth strong muscles of his back and go instinctively to the one spot I know will tell him what I need. I cup the two velvety mounds of his rock-hard ass and urge him to enter me. It's an invitation he can't resist because he adjusts his shaft, placing the soft head at my entrance. I'm already one inch from exploding. *More like eight inches.*

"Don't stop," I pant.

He hesitates for a moment, but then thrusts his hips and enters me with one smooth stroke.

I let out a moan. It's so much better this time. "More."

He withdraws and then sharply thrusts again. He breaks our kiss and watches me climbing toward the edge. Higher and higher. His pace becomes a steady rhythm of deep penetrations. He's thick and long, and every movement of his cock creates the most delicious friction. Meanwhile, his mouth moves to my neck, and his hands massage my breasts and stroke my outer thighs. His body writhes with pleasure, working over me, and my skin feels like a giant blanket of tingles. He's everywhere—inside me, covering my body, and beating through my heart.

"I love you," I whisper, unable to articulate the blissful sensation any other way.

Suddenly, I'm combusting, my body shattering into a hundred carnal contractions that paralyze me. He's relentless with his pistoning hips as I come, hammering out every last orgasmic spasm.

"Fuck." He groans so loud his voice echoes through the bedroom. I feel his cock twitch inside me, releasing his cum, and it sparks one more delicious wave of euphoria.

Panting, he begins moving slowly while kissing me. I love the feel of his bare slick cock stroking my sensitive bud, and I don't ever want this to end because as unaccustomed as I am to intimacy—a man being inside me, holding me, kissing me—I know there's nothing more beautiful than this. Being with the right man.

He stops kissing me for a moment and stares into my eyes. "I choose the bear."

"What?"

He cracks a smile. "He's really cute. So…"

"Ha-ha. Very funny."

His smile melts away. "You know I love you, Georgie."

I bob my head. "Yeah. I do."

"Good. Because if we're going to make this work, you can't have any doubts."

I know he's not just talking about him and me. There's Joy, too. And despite my inexperience with kids, I know it will be a challenge learning how to be a part of their family. But I love Sam and I know I'll love his little girl. That's all I need.

"You can't have any doubts either," I say, "because you'll be part of my family, too."

The warmth in Sam's eyes dissipates while that plays out in his head. Henry still wants to kill him. "I look forward to not dying."

# CHAPTER TWENTY-EIGHT

*Six Months Later.*

It's our first Christmas together as a new family, and oh boy, where do I start?

My father was proven to be a major asshole, but sane, and is now serving thirty years in prison. Henry and I testified at the trial, and though I thought I would feel some sense of closure, I realized that a part of me will always hurt. It can't be helped. A child, no matter how old, will always wonder why her father didn't love him or her enough to make a different choice. The irony for me, and maybe for my siblings, too, is that it's made us all so grateful for the love we do have. We're closer than we ever were.

Michelle and Chewy are expecting their first baby in the spring. Claire, my oldest sister, is single but has decided to adopt and is currently on several waiting lists. She says her perfect man will have to fit in with her life and not the other way around—perhaps a result of growing up with Chester Walton, who tried to bend and mold us to fit into his life.

My mother is officially divorced, single, and likely to remain so, but I don't know if she's happy or sad about it. Georgina Walton Senior is not the sort of woman to show weakness, but she does show kindness in her own way.

"Come here, you little rat," my mother says with a smile on her face while she makes claws at Joy. "I'm going to eat you."

"Mom," I warn.

"What?" My mom gives me a look. "Have you ever seen a cuter little girl? I just want to eat her up!"

Joy, who's wearing a red dress and has her dark curly hair in pigtails, laughs. My mother swoops her up and carries her off to the kitchen to check on dinner, which she's decided to cook herself this year. It's weird not having caterers, wait staff, and two hundred of my parents' "closest" friends, like we did for years, but I love our new "family only" tradition.

*And our new and improved family.* Which will only get better with time, especially since we started selling off all of the companies except for Elle's baby, Algae-Tech, and PVP. Elle and Henry, who is now officially playing for the NFL, decided to keep PVP in order to make sure things keep running smoothly and the medicines get to where they are needed. We even started a charity under Sam's wife's name to help cancer patients with other medical costs, such as doctor visits and housing, while they undergo treatments. A lot of good has come out of my father's misdeeds, which I know is a bigger punishment for him than sitting in a jail cell for the next three decades. He must hate knowing we're spending "his" fortune on others.

I smile at Sam, who's sitting on the couch beside me in a black sweater and jeans, looking sexier than ever. His posture is less stiff these days, but he's always on his guard, forever the protective man I love.

"So, I have some news," Sam says to me. "I finally found a new job."

"Really?" He took a long, long few months off to spend time with Joy. Okay, and with me. Then Erin, his sister-in-law, had her wedding, which we helped out with. Then Sam and I bought a really nice house in a neighborhood an equal distance from the university and from my mom and Claire's. Erin and her new hubby, Logan, are at Sam's old house, which they're renting from him while they start out.

Anyway, between all that, the trial, starting up at school again, and Sam getting used to being with a woman who is rich, wants to be a lawyer, and is continuing to find herself, well, it's been a wild, insane journey. His consolation is that I make him have sex with me a lot. I mean, *a lot*. I can't get enough of him, and he loves it. The man is constantly walking around with a big fat smile.

"So what's the job?" I ask.

"I'm starting my own company. High-profile,

celebrity security."

*Huh?* "You're going to be a bodyguard?"

He nods.

"That is so hot." I literally see him wearing his sexy badass suit, those mirrored sunglasses, and saying things like *Hurt her and I'll break your thumbs.* He knows how to be scary.

"My first client will be Mitch."

"The Bulge?" My jaw drops.

Sam's eyes narrow. "How do you know about his nickname?"

"It's only been in a thousand tabloids." I laugh. "So why a bodyguard? Why not sales or something? You were so good at all that."

"Not really. All those rumors of my success were made up. Even my references were fake—compliments of the FBI."

*Huh. Interesting.* I suppose I'm not shocked. I already know he didn't go to Yale, though after serving in the Marines, he did get a business degree from Dartmouth in New Hampshire, where he's originally from. Later, he got a master's in criminology and joined the FBI.

"So how did you know so much about sales?" Because he certainly had me convinced.

"I took a job selling industrial equipment after I got my business degree. My boss taught me everything I know."

*Wow.* "Why didn't you ever mention this?" Not that we talk much about the past. It's sort of an unsaid rule between us. We're in love and we've committed to a fresh start together. So while the past can't be completely avoided, we choose to look forward. For both our sakes and for Joy's.

He shrugs.

*Oh no. He only shrugs when it's bad.* "Sam?"

"I met Kate there."

"Oh."

"After she passed away, I went back to school and applied for the bureau." He looks away, across the room. I can tell by his tightly knit brows that he feels uncomfortable talking about this.

"Sam, I know we've focused on moving on, but please don't ever feel like you can't talk about her. She's a part of you and Joy, and I happen to love you both very much."

He spears me with those intense eyes. "I love you. You know that, right?"

I nod.

"Good, because I don't want you to think that I'm not all in with you."

"Okay." I don't think that, but I do wonder what he's getting at.

"So when the time is right, you know that I'm going to ask you."

It takes a moment for me to read between the lines.

*Marriage.* My heart goes into pitter-patter mode. I can't imagine my life without him, and Joy has become this unexpected ray of sunshine in my life. She's not only smart, funny, and adventurous, but I'm getting a second chance at a happy childhood, living vicariously through her. She's got more love than she knows what to do with, and she won't ever feel like she doesn't matter. Sam would never let that happen to her.

"The answer will be yes." I peck Sam on the lips.

"Good. I just wanted to wait until the press and everything died down. I want the moment to be perfect."

I grin. "I'm good with that." As long as we're together, I can wait for the rose petals, champagne, and the man I love bending his knee. After all, you only marry the man of your dreams once.

"So, bodyguarding. It's great news. When do you start?" I squeeze his hand.

"After the holidays. I've actually recruited my first employee to help with Mitch's surveillance: Your friend Abi."

"Huh?" My eyes go wide. "Abi? My Abi?"

"What's wrong with her? She's smart. She wanted the job, and I need someone who will blend in with Mitch's mostly female entourage."

Besides the fact she has zero training in anything remotely related to self-defense or defense of others and is—or was until recently—the second most shy person on the planet? *Ummm…*

"She hates Mitch. With a passion. He apparently slept with her at that party we went to and then tossed her out on her ass the next morning." And she refuses to talk about it even with me. I love her, so I've respected her wishes, but I know it took her months to get over it. He was her first. *What a dick. A big dick.*

"Oh." Sam scratches the scruff on his jaw.

"Yeah, 'oh.' Does she know her first job will be guarding that manwhore?"

Sam frowns. "Well, I guess I'll have to find someone else."

But Abi's internship is over, and she needs the job. She was just telling me how desperate she is for money to pay for her final semester. Of course, I offered to loan her money, but she won't take it.

"Better let her decide," I say. "Maybe she's fine with it, and if she's not, maybe she wants to be. Abi always surprises me with her choices."

"Have I ever told you how much I love your positivity?"

"Maybe, but tell me again," I say.

"I love it. And I love you." The adoration in his eyes undoes me every time. It's not just that he makes me feel special and safe, but that he believes in me. He pushes me every day to overcome every hurdle I encounter, be it dealing with the press, trying to make my way through school as a person who is now recognized as much as my father, or just being a woman with huge aspirations. Sam is there, loving me and refusing to let me be anything less than I am: a smart, capable woman.

"Sam, you have no idea what you do to me."

He shakes his head. "You're the one who's been driving me crazy since we first met."

I frown. "What are you talking about?"

"Oh, don't pretend you didn't notice me drooling all over you—those tight skirts and sweet little lips. The way you looked at me with your sexy green eyes."

My skirts were just skirts. Okay, they were a little tight because I'm slightly curvier than Claire, but they weren't *that* sexy. "I had no clue."

He whispers in my ear, "And that red dress you wore to the fundraiser. I couldn't get you out of my mind. I don't think I've ever had to jerk off so many times to keep my head straight."

I blink at him. The thought of him leaning back, his cock in his hand while he—

*Christmas. Family. Children present.* "Change subject fast," I blurt out.

He grins, knowing full well what he's doing to me. "Did I ever tell you," he keeps whispering in my ear, "how hard you made me when you were sitting next to me in my office and—"

"You are a wicked man, Sam," I mutter under my breath. "Let's meet upstairs in five minutes."

"Sorry. You have to wait until we're home tonight," he murmurs seductively. "But know I'll be thinking about all the ways I'm going to fuck you once we're alone."

"Oh," I give him a look, "you are a cruel, cruel man." And I can't wait that long for him. I take his hand. "Just two minutes in the bathroom upstairs."

Sam's about to tell me to keep it in my horny lady-pants when my phone rings. It's Henry. *Oh*

*God! I almost forgot!*

My hands fumble to answer. "Hello?"

"Georgie, tell everyone it's a girl!" Henry sounds like he's crying.

My eyes tear, and I can't speak. I'm just so happy. *I'm an auntie!*

Noticing I'm in a happy, emotional lockdown, Sam takes the phone from my hand and hands it to my sister Claire. "I think it's good news." He passes it off, and I hear my sisters screaming out the wonderful news to my mom.

Sam leans over and whispers in my ear, "I love you, Georgie. Thank you for bringing happiness back into my life." He kisses my cheek, and I take a deep breath. It's not the end of our story. It's just the beginning. Because I so, so dig this man.

## THE END

Looking for more of the OHellNo series? *BATTLE OF THE BULGE* is coming next! (Sneak peek of the cover is on the next page.) Don't miss it. Sign up for Mimi Jean's very magical newsletter (it magically appears when new books come out) or check here www.mimijean.net/bulge.html for updates, buy links, and extras.

## AND...

KEEP READING FOR instructions on how to get a free signed bookmark!

# AUTHOR'S NOTE

Hello, my awesome nerds, jocks, bookworms, romance fans, innocent bystanders, introverts, extroverts, and a-hole fans (I mean that figuratively, though I'm not judging).

I hope you enjoyed Georgie and Sam, but most of all, I hope I made you laugh. I won't lie, I couldn't stop chuckling when coming up with Nick's creative insults (Dumpster in a skirt? Hehe. I mean, it's just so wrong). But, of course, I followed his sales technique—start with the worst possible scenario and finish with the good!—hoping to make you walk away loving him as much as I did. (What a sweet jerkface!)

Anyway, up next is an epic love war. THE BATTLE OF THE BULGE…

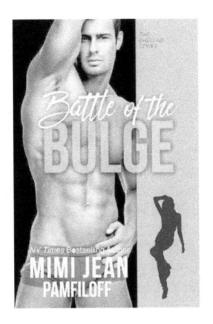

Sizzle. Sizzle. CHECK HERE FOR UPDATES: www.mimijean.net/bulge.html or sign up for my newsletter for an alert. Sign up for Mimi's mailing list for giveaways and new release news!

If you're looking for a SIGNED *DIGGING A HOLE* BOOKMARK & MAGNET:

1. Email me with your shipping address. (Include country, *por favor.*)
2. If you took the time to show the book-love with a review, thank you! You rock for supporting your favorite authors! No matter how big a writer gets, she/he is ultimately engaging in a very personal relationship. You are letting us into your hearts and minds. So don't ever feel

like your appreciation is meaningless. As for me, I like to show my reader-love. Provide a link or screen shot of your review in your email. (Magnets are on a first-come basis, so I do run out, but at the very least you'll get a wonderful thank-you from me!)

3. Draw upon your pity for me as I sign 1K+ bookmarks and then endeavor to stuff them into envelopes.

4. Keep a lookout for a confirmation email from me. (Don't hate me, but sometimes it takes about one month to get to all of them.) If you don't hear from me by then, assume the spam-monster has eaten your email.

While you're waiting, you can always listen to my crazy DIGGING A HOLE PLAYLIST here:

https://open.spotify.com/user/mimijeanpamfiloff/playlist/3zagS0Zpb90nzgBPbs9uXA?si=FC_7bHTyS7 GWLGzynk5yvw.

I especially recommend the "ASSHOLE" song by Dennis Leary. I think it channels the spirit of Craigson perfectly. What a super asshole.

As for my semi-regular book breakdown, I think it would be an insult to your intelligence to explain what the book meant. I can only add that while I'm probably a six or seven on the extrovert scale, I think most of us have a little Georgie in us. She's the piece that, at one time or another, kept our mouths closed when we really wanted to be fighting. In the end, however, maybe what defines us isn't the times we stayed quiet, but the times we spoke up. No one can be "on" all the time. No one can fight every battle and horrible person they come across. We have to choose; otherwise we'd spend our entire lives as a species pissed off and fighting. In my humble opinion, we're all better off focusing 90% of our time on the good—love, family, friendship—which fuels our hearts and souls. And when we have to fight, we fight because it's right and our calling.

I call for more love!

XOXO,
*Mimi*

## ACKNOWLEDGEMENTS

You're all warrior squirrels for *digging* in and helping out with book #33! Which is why I love you. So thank you for putting up with this major a-hole/fiction maniac/romance rebel who can't seem to stop herself from going for the warrior-squirrelly plot twists!

So to Su, Karen, Dali, Ally, Latoya, Pauline, and Paul: I dig you. Thank you!

To my dudes: I dig you, too, but please stop washing my colors with bleach and the whites with the darks. My clothes look like they belong to a criminally insane person. I'm only a bit crazy. ☺

With Love,
Mimi

## Upcoming Releases!
## CHECK

Book Three and the Finale of the Sexy, Suspenseful
Mr. Rook's Island.

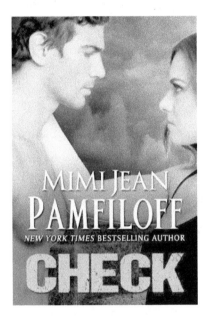

FOR MORE, GO TO:

www.mimijean.net/check.html

# THE LIBRARIAN'S VAMPIRE ASSISTANT

Book 2

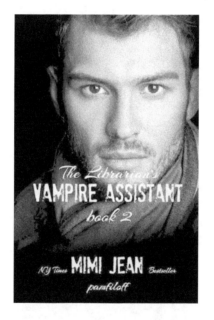

FOR MORE, GO TO:

www.mimijean.net/the-librarians-vampire-assistant-2.html

## LOOKING FOR A DARK ADVENTURE?

**Check out *Mr. Rook's Island*, a Sexy, Romantic Suspense.**

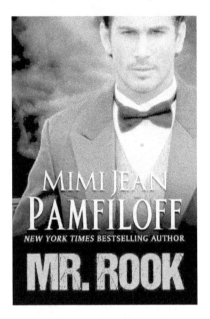

**He's Enigmatic, Dangerously Handsome, and COMPLETELY OFF-LIMITS...**

The women who vacation on Mr. Rook's exclusive island are looking for one thing and one thing only: to have their wildest romantic fantasies come to life. Pirates, cowboys, billionaires—there's nothing

Rook's staff can't deliver.

But when Stephanie Fitzgerald's sister doesn't return after her week in paradise, Stephanie will have to pose as a guest in order to dig for answers. Unfortunately, this means she'll need to get close to the one thing on the island that's not on the menu: the devastatingly handsome and intimidating Mr. Rook. And he's not about to give the island's secrets away.

FOR MORE, GO TO:

www.mimijean.net/rooksisland.html

or continue reading for an excerpt.

# EXCERPT MR. ROOK
## PROLOGUE

My name is Stephanie Fitzgerald. I am twenty-six years old, London born, New York raised, and I know exactly three things about my current situation.

One: I am an imposter riding on this private jet carrying myself and eleven other women to an island "paradise."

Two: I have no clue what I will find when I disembark, because this exclusive resort doesn't exactly advertise.

Three: I will be fired if I don't return home with concrete information regarding Mr. Rook, the mysterious owner of the island. And when I say I'll be fired, I really mean that my body will be thrown down a deep dark well by a bad, bad man.

Those three things, however, don't really matter. Only finding my sister does. Because the last place Cici was seen alive is here, "Fantasy Island." Yep, that's what some people actually call it. Some even say the show in the '80s was based on this place.

*Sure. If your fantasy is to disappear, leaving your family an emotional train wreck, then okay, I concede the point.*

Regardless, this is where Cici went after winning a mystery dream vacation in the back of some travel magazine, and it's touted as the real deal. You pay fifty K. They make your wildest fantasies come true. One week in Heaven.

*Heaven, my ass.*

As the tires hit the wet landing strip and the plane slows to a crawl, I glance out the tiny oval window to my left, and my breath hitches. Standing among the lush vegetation lining the runway is a tall man with square shoulders. He's looking right at me, and those eyes—so predatory, so cold—are the only thing I can really see of him.

I blink, and he vanishes like a wisp of steam.

*Fuck. What was that?* A hard shiver slams through me as I realize I have no clue what I've just gotten myself into. Because I am one of the next happy guests at Mr. Rook's private island, where "Every woman's fantasy is our business." *And not everyone comes home from vacation.*

# CHAPTER ONE

Like its mysterious owner, Rook's Island was practically an urban legend. No brochures. No real website. They advertised strictly by *whisper* of mouth. In other words, you had to know someone willing to tell you about it. Confidentially.

But from the bits and pieces I'd gathered off the Internet, I deduced it was an uncharted island somewhere west of the Bermuda Triangle in Bahaman waters, likely northwest of Highborne Cay among a cluster of unnamed isles. That said, no one could tell you exactly where it was, and if they knew, they'd never admit it. Even the employees of the Bahaman government had simply stared at me like I was a madwoman.

"There is nothing in those waters, ma'am, except fish," one of the clerks from the Bahaman embassy in DC had said several months ago.

"Then why the hell did my sister have a *goddamned* plane ticket to the island?"

The man had simply shrugged. "I cannot say, ma'am. I have never heard of such a place, so perhaps your sister simply lied. People disappear on purpose all the time."

*What the fuck?* Cici, my sister, was a goddamned saint, a kindergarten teacher who loved her life. She lived for those kids and was the kind of person who made everyone smile.

*Unlike me.* I used to be outgoing and optimistic, but now I'm just broken. I'm broken because I loved my big sister more than anything. She was my best friend, my blood, and my hero. She was there for me when my widowed father was too busy working and I was trying to grow up without a mother. Cici made us a family, and now she was gone. Just like that. A fact the police had little to say about since they had a video of her clearing out her safe deposit box.

"She did not abandon us, you piece of shit!" I had screamed at the embassy guy. "Now help me fucking find her!"

The rest of that moment—a blur, really—consisted of multiple expletives, resulting in my being arrested and banned from their embassy. Indefinitely. My father, an award-winning war correspondent, had to pull a few strings to get me out of jail that day.

"Stephanie, please don't do this to me," he'd said, his thinning gray hair its usual mess, his strong hands wrapped tightly around the steering wheel of his Volvo—an old beige thing he'd purchased for my mother right before she died. God rest her beautiful soul. She had been a journalist like my dad when they met in Afghanistan, but they moved around a lot for work, eventually landing in New York right after I came along. Then one morning, she was out for a jog and dropped dead of a heart attack. Poof. Gone forever from our lives.

My poor father was never right in the head again, and until this day, he refused to let go of my mom or that Volvo. So while I never really knew her, I felt the painful void she'd left behind, which was why I couldn't give up searching for Cici or accept that there was no island.

*And look. There it is...* I glanced out the tiny window of the plane, knowing I was one step closer to getting answers.

My heart hammered against my rib cage as the private jet's outer door popped open. Okay, really, my heart hadn't stopped hammering since I'd boarded. What kind of place doesn't require a visa or passport? *A shady place, that's what.*

"Ladies," said the stewardess with dark brown hair matching my own, "the staff here at Mr. Rook's island would like to welcome you to your dream vacation. As you exit the plane, please be careful descending the staircase. Of course," she giggled, "if you do decide to fall, there will be a strong, handsome gentleman waiting to catch you."

The female passengers, who'd been sipping fancy cocktails since we boarded at a private airfield south of Newark, started clapping and hooting.

"I'm definitely taking a dive, then!" barked out a redhead in her mid-forties, wearing an animal print blouse, white jeggings, and a heavy amount of gold jewelry around her neck. Her accent screamed Southerner, while her outfit screamed new money and that she liked borrowing clothes from her daughter—the one she'd been talking about nonstop to the other passenger directly behind me. Apparently, the redhead had just got divorced from her wealthy cheating husband and the daughter recently graduated from college. This vacation was her big indulgence after years of marital ugliness. The woman to her side, a timid little blonde thing, didn't say much other than her sister had come to Rook's Island over a decade ago and hadn't stop talking about it since.

"I can't wait to meet Mr. Rook," said the redhead. "I hear he's the most delicious thing on the island."

"My sister only saw him once because he didn't mingle much with the guests," said the blonde lady.

"Well," said the redhead with a sassy voice, "if he's as good looking as my friends say, I'm changing my fantasy to a night with him."

In the back of my mind, I tried to understand how these women could actually pay money to come all the way here and sleep with strange men in a weeklong, role-playing, fantasy vacation. It felt so strange to me.

"What's your fantasy this week, sweetheart?" the

redhead asked, staring at me with her mascara-caked eyes.

"Who, me?" I pointed to my chest.

"Yeah. You gonna do some pirate fantasy? Oh wait. I know. You look like the superhero kind." She snapped her fingers. "Thor. You went for the Thor fantasy, didn't ya? I heard he has the biggest *hammer* in the world." She winked.

*Nice. Real nice.* And why had she made that assessment about me? My look didn't scream cosplay-lover. It didn't scream anything, really. Most men—my exes—would describe me as having classic beauty. I would describe myself as average. Average-length brown hair with average waves. Average brown eyes. Average five foot four height. Average ten pounds overweight. Average intelligence.

My special feature was my tenacity. Once I set out to do something, I achieved my goal no matter how difficult. For example, when I was eight and Cici was fourteen, I decided that our yard needed a treehouse. My father said he was too busy, so I put up a lemonade stand every weekend for five months until I raised enough money to hire a handyman. I got my damned treehouse.

I smiled politely at the redhead and mousy blonde who waited for my reply. "I, uh, really just want flowers, a candlelit dinner on a yacht, and cuddling by the fire—your basic romance," I lied.

They looked at me like I was out of my soft skull for choosing something so tame. But I wasn't here for wild. I was here to find Cici.

"Well, that's cute," said the redhead.

"I'm doing Tarzan," said the blonde, staring at the floor.

I tried to keep a straight face. I couldn't picture this shy little thing swinging through the trees in a suede bikini.

"Sounds…" I swallowed, "dangerous."

"I knooow." Her brown eyes lit with joy.

The line began to clear out of the cabin, so I grabbed my backpack and purse and faced forward.

"Well, enjoy your romantic candles…?" Redhead wanted to know my name.

I glanced over my shoulder. "Stephanie."

"Nice to meet you. I'm Meg," she said and then jerked her head toward the blonde, "and she's Emily."

"Nice meeting you, too," I replied politely.

"We'll see you at the welcome dinner tonight!" Meg said. "I hear the dancers are amazing—ripped from head to toe and almost naked in those Hawaiian grass skirt things."

"Mmmm. Can't wait." I didn't give a crap about dancers or dinners. I wanted to find this Mr. Rook and start asking about Cici. I was ready to put a goddamned knife to his throat if that was what it took.

"Right this way, ladies!" said the overly peppy air stewardess.

One by one, we filed down the rollaway staircase. I immediately noticed the tropical summer heat, the never-ending stretch of lush green jungle, and the musty smell of moist dirt mixed with salty air.

My mind immediately jumped to my sister— her bright smile and big brown eyes. She had been right here on this island, on this very fucking staircase. *What did they do to her?*

My heart bubbled with rage. *Stay in character, Steph. You're a happy guest, like everyone else.* The last thing I wanted was to go ballistic and get kicked off the island before I got what I needed—the truth for myself and information for "my boss," Warner Price. I used the term loosely because Warner and I had more of an arrangement rather than an employer-employee situation. Either way, I couldn't and wouldn't go home until I had what I needed.

Wearing black leather sandals and a long blue cotton dress, I carefully descended the narrow staircase, feeling my anxiety well inside my shaky knees.

"Welcome, Miss…?" Holding out his hand, next to the bottom step, stood a huge tree trunk of a man wearing a blue-and-white Hawaiian shirt and khaki shorts. He had to be at least seven feet tall, his brown skin covered in Samoan tattoos. Even his neck and the back of his shaved head were inked.

"Ms. Brenna," I lied, and shook his large hand. "Let me guess. You must be Tattoo and you tell everyone when the plane arrives?" *This place is a fucking joke.*

He smiled and flashed a set of bright white teeth. "My name is Gerry, ma'am, and our control tower texts the employees to alert us when the guests arrive. May I help you with your things?"

"No." I smiled politely, smoothing down the front of my wrinkled dress, trying my best not to show him the hate inside me. Because for all I knew, he'd had something to do with Cici's death.

*No. Don't think that. She's not dead.* Sadly, however, my heart knew she would not leave us. Not like that. Which naturally led to one conclusion: She never made it off this island alive.

I held back a snarl and substituted it with a grin. "I can carry my own things, but thanks."

"Very good, Ms. Brenna." Tattoo—I mean Gerry—dipped his shaved head. "Please follow the red carpet to the gravel path. The signs will direct you to the reception building, where our staff will check you in."

"Thanks."

Gerry turned his attention to the next guest behind me—Meg—and I continued on the red carpet, squinting from the hot summer sun beating down on the top of my head.

My first impression of the place was that everything felt too perfect, like a movie set or theme park. Yes, the tall trees were real, and the birds of paradise sprouting from beds of bright red and yellow flowers were real, too, but even the gravel path I followed through the dense jungle didn't have a single pebble out of place.

As I walked, the muted giggles and laughter of the ladies behind me echoed through the trees. All I felt was my skin crawling and those eyes—from the shadow—still watching me.

*Stop it*, I told myself. *You're letting your imagination get to you.*

I slid my cell from my purse to check for texts or messages from my dad. *Crap. No bars? Not even one little flicker?* I guess I wasn't surprised. This island couldn't stay a secret if people were posting their location on Facebook along with vacation pics.

After a very short walk, the shaded path ended at a large, two-story house with an enormous porch and hanging flowers of every color imaginable. It reminded me of those old coffee plantation homes with whitewash paint and pillars.

I walked up the steps to the porch, my body already dripping with sweat. "Jesus, this place is like living inside a wet volcano," I muttered. I couldn't say I was a fan of humidity before this and now I absolutely loathed it.

I stepped inside the house, where a gentle breeze from the ceiling fans drifted against my hot skin, giving some relief. The white wood-paneled room had fresh flowers atop two white desks, where two pleasant-looking women awaited us. *Oh, look. We're being checked in to heaven.* Every perfect detail of this shitty place pissed me off.

The guests formed a line and then gave their names to the women in blue-and-white blouses behind the desks. After that, another woman, different every time, quickly whisked them off down a hallway.

*My turn.* I stepped up, feeling nervous as hell. I wasn't great at lying, but there was no other way. *I'm a guest. A happy guest.*

"Hi. I'm Stephanie Brenna."

The young woman with cocoa skin and her black hair pulled into a neat ponytail smiled and then checked my name off her list. "There you are, Ms. Brenna. Julie will be checking you in and going over the island's amenities and rules during your stay."

Julie, a brunette wearing white shorts and the standard Hawaiian blouse, appeared with a bright smile. "Ms. Brenna, hello. Please come right this way."

"What is this?" The whole whisking people away and separating the guests made me uneasy.

The receptionist continued smiling like she was high on life or had just gotten her wings. "Ah, yes. Well, our check-in process is a little different than your standard resort." She leaned into her desk and whispered, "Because of the *unique* nature of our services." She winked.

"So you mean there's sex paperwork," I said.

She pointed her pencil at me. "You got it. And a safety orientation."

"And Mr. Rook? When do I get to meet him?" I asked.

The smiles on the women's faces melted so fast, one might have assumed I'd just told them I'd like to eat their livers.

"What?" I asked. "This is his island, isn't it?"

Julie, my check-in hostess, swallowed something in her throat. "I'm afraid that Mr. Rook doesn't manage the day-to-day operations of the island— he's a very busy man. However, if you have any concerns or needs—anything at all—I will be your personal concierge for the week." Her fake smile reappeared. "And if there's anything I can't manage, the island's executive manager, Mrs. Day, can see to it."

"So I won't get to meet the famous Mr. Rook?" I asked.

They smiled politely, but didn't speak. I got the distinct impression that they were not allowed to say no to a guest.

"All right. Is he even on the island?" I prodded.

The receptionist offered me a bone. "Mr. Rook does have a personal residence here, but we are not kept informed of his schedule or whereabouts. Is there anything we can address? Any concerns?"

The two women eyed the line of rowdy drunk guests behind me. Apparently, one of them had to pee, a fact she happily shared with us all.

Okay, well, if Mr. Rook didn't run things on a daily basis, then he wasn't the only person with answers. Of course, the big boss would have to know if a guest went missing, so I would still need to meet him.

"No." I flashed a smile to make nice. "No concerns at this time."

"Then follow me!" Julie turned for the hallway. "In a few short minutes, I'll have you on your way to a week of pure pampering and relaxation."

"Fabulous." I followed behind her.

"Unless your version of relaxation requires something more vigorous." She glanced over her shoulder and winked.

*What's with the damned winking?* This entire place gave me the heebie-jeebies. "Can't wait."

## FOR MORE:

www.mimijean.net/rooksisland.html

## LIKE MYSTERIES AND LAUGHS?

Check Out This Horribly Sunny Mystery, *The Librarian's Vampire Assistant.*

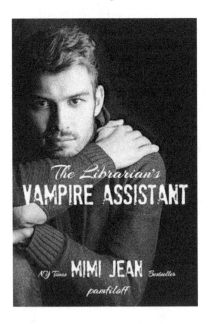

## NOBODY MESSES WITH HIS LIBRARIAN. . .

Who killed Michael Vanderhorst's maker? It's a darn good question. But when the trail brings Michael to hellishly sunny Phoenix, Arizona, his biggest problem soon becomes a cute little librarian he can't seem to stay away from. He's never met a bigger danger magnet! Even her book cart has it out for her. And is that the drug cartel following her around, too? "Dear God, woman! What have you gotten yourself into?"

Things go from bad to worse when local vampires won't play nice.

Can this four-hundred-year-old vampire keep his librarian safe and himself out of hot water? Can he bring his maker's killer to justice? Yesterday, he would've said yes. But yesterday, he didn't have a strange connection with a librarian. Yesterday, people weren't trying to kill her.

FOR MORE, GO TO:

www.mimijean.net/the-librarians-vampire-assistant.html

or continue reading for an excerpt.

# EXCERPT THE LIBRARIAN'S VAMPIRE ASSISTANT
## CHAPTER ONE

"Oh! I'm so sorry!" says a blonde at the front of the coffee line, forcing my attention away from the phone in my hand. She's wearing a rather unattractive red coat and has apparently rammed into a UPS guy carrying a hot cup of tea.

"Serves him right. Only weak men drink tea," I growl under my breath and return to my screen.

My name is Michael Vanderhorst, and I am not usually this grouchy or this close to doing something terribly unwise—throats torn, heads lopped, appendages removed. Unwise. However, today is quite possibly the worst day of my life, and a silent rage is brewing inside me.

But let us not start off on the wrong foot. I am actually a nice guy. Some might say I'm a classic gentleman, and they don't mean I know which fork to use, though I do. They mean *gentleman* in the true, old-fashioned sense. I open doors for ladies and stand when they rise from the table. I keep my word, pay my debts, and believe in being polite to others, even when they don't deserve it.

Do not get the wrong impression. I am no pushover either. I get my hands dirty when the situation warrants, but generally I am an agreeable man.

Or I used to be.

A man.

Now I'm a vampire, and like most of my kind, the journey hasn't been an easy one.

No, this is not the reason I'm in a foul mood. Neither is the fact that I've been in line for over ten minutes, waiting to order coffee.

*Oh, yes*—pause of deep appreciation—*coffee*.

"Oh, dear me! I'm so sorry!" I look up again, and the same blonde woman, who I see only from the back, has just knocked over a towering pile of coffee cup lids onto the floor.

The employees rush to pick up the mess, and when she bends over to help, she hits her forehead on the counter. "Ouch!"

I am about to step forward to assist, but she seems all right, rubbing her head and apologizing to the entire world.

*I hope she doesn't stab herself with a straw or spontaneously combust. Then I'll never get my coffee.* I cannot start my day without it.

Do not be shocked. There are many things people don't know about my kind. For example, we don't live exclusively on blood. In fact, I prefer spicy vegan dishes. Indian food is delicious.

Another myth? Vampires cannot go in the sun. Also untrue. We are merely averse to it. Right now, it's a cool spring morning in downtown Phoenix, and while I am sweating through my Italian suit and can't get home to Cincinnati fast enough, the sunny sky outside is merely an annoyance.

So now you're wondering just why I'm so angry. It is something so ghastly, I can hardly say the words. Two days ago, someone killed the most upstanding person ever to walk the planet. Clive was a give-you-the-shirt-off-his-back sort of man, which is the likely reason his detective agency wasn't making money. I once worked for Clive—also a vampire—but his generosity toward his clients, giving away his services, got to a point where he could no longer employ me.

So I went back to school, obtained yet another degree, and started my eighth profession, this time in biotech research. When you've lived as long as I have, you get bored. I find changing occupations every fifty years keeps a man on his toes, and if you've guessed that would make me over four hundred years old, you would be correct.

"It's your turn, dude," says the pink-haired man behind me.

"About time. Thank you." I step up to the counter, where I order my usual—a nonfat latte with an extra shot of espresso. "No make that two extra shots," I say to the barista and pop five dollars into the tip jar.

"Coming right up." The young redhead attending to me smiles, but it's the sort of smile that says she wants to bed me. Little does she know that while I am a handsome man—six feet one, deep brown eyes, and a very charming smile—she can't help herself. Yes, *that* myth is actually true. Humans find us irresistible.

I offer the barista a polite nod and step aside to await my coffee, but something outside catches my eye through the plate-glass window. It's that same blonde woman with a paper cup in her hand, playing *Frogger* with oncoming traffic.

*Oh! Watch out. Dear woman, what are you doing!* She's nearly run over by three separate cars. I'm about to run after her, but she makes it across to the other side of the street.

*What the devil was she thinking?*

My cell vibrates in my hand, and I sigh with relief. "Finally." It's a text from the local society granting me a meeting at one o'clock. *Society* is the modern term for *coven*, which is made up of a collection of families. Each territory has a different society and, since vampires are very territorial, I cannot stay longer than a day without a visa—not that I plan to since I'm not permitted to have anything to do with investigating Clive's death.

Sadly, I am here to collect Clive's ashes and take the good man home to his final resting place.

Regardless, whoever hurt him must pay. Not death, but entombment, which is far worse and the only outcome I'm expecting to hear at today's meeting with the society's head. "*We've caught the bastard. He's been sentenced to life.*" Anything shy of these exact words will cause trouble. From me.

My order is called at the counter, and I grab my hot coffee, immediately going in for that first delicious sip. "Ow!" It burns my tongue. *Why do I always do that?* I'm far too eager when it comes to caffeine. Especially in the morning.

I take a seat at the counter along the window that faces the street. Immediately, my reflection catches my eye. My brown hair is a mess, and I apparently forgot to shave this morning at the hotel. My tie is also crooked.

I straighten myself out and glance at my watch, a fine antique Clive gave me on my birthday over a hundred years ago.

*Clive…* I feel the red-hot rage build again. He was my best friend, my brother, my father, and my maker.

*Nobody touches my family*, I snarl on the inside. My strong hand squeezes my coffee cup, threatening to send the piping hot liquid up in the air.

*Dammit all to hell.* I need a distraction, something to keep me calm until one o'clock. Otherwise, I won't stand a chance of keeping a level head when I walk in to meet whoever runs this sunny, pleasant dump of a town.

My eyes gravitate back outside. I remember passing a library one block down. I'm sure I can find a quiet place there to get some work done on my laptop, which will keep me out of the sun and occupied for the next few hours.

With coffee in one hand, I grab my things and head to the library.

FOR BUY LINKS AND MORE:

www.mimijean.net/the-librarians-vampire-assistant

# ABOUT THE AUTHOR

MIMI JEAN PAMFILOFF is a *New York Times* bestselling author who's sold over one million books around the world. Although she obtained her MBA and worked for more than fifteen years in the corporate world, she believes that it's never too late to come out of the romance closet and follow your dream. Mimi lives with her Latin lover hubby, two pirates-in-training (their boys), and the rat terrier duo, Snowflake and Mini Me, in Arizona. She hopes to make you laugh when you need it most and continues to pray daily that leather pants will make a big comeback for men.

Sign up for Mimi's mailing list for giveaways and new release news!